OTHERWISE ENGAGED

Lord Mottesford wagers he can bring Prudence to heel, but she resists his blandishments. He should help his cousin Charlotte, poor and threatened with dreadful Hubert, while her stepmother, the former cook, seeks a wealthy husband for her daughter Emma. Introducing Charlotte to acceptable men, Prudence forgets the wager. She believes Mottesford's astonishing proposal, but when he is trapped into a betrothal with Emma, Prudence realises her love for him.

Books by Sally James
in the Linford Romance Library:

A CLANDESTINE AFFAIR
MIRANDA OF THE ISLAND
MASK OF FORTUNE

SALLY JAMES

OTHERWISE ENGAGED

Complete and Unabridged

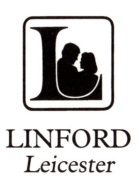

LINFORD
Leicester

First published in Great Britain

First Linford Edition
published 2001

British Library CIP Data

James, Sally, *1934* –
 Otherwise engaged.—Large print ed.—
 Linford romance library
 1. Love stories
 2. Large type books
 I. Title
 823.9'14 [F]

 ISBN 0–7089–4551–1

Published by
F. A. Thorpe (Publishing)
Anstey, Leicestershire

Set by Words & Graphics Ltd.
Anstey, Leicestershire
Printed and bound in Great Britain by
T. J. International Ltd., Padstow, Cornwall

This book is printed on acid-free paper

1

Prudence halted so abruptly that her cousin Netta, chattering busily about her plans for the following day, did not immediately realise that she had walked on alone. She turned round to find Prudence searching anxiously through the packages she was holding.

'Pru, have you dropped something?' she asked with a hint of impatience in her tone.

'Netta, I think I must have left those silks in the shop which your mama particularly asked me to match. I shall have to go back for them.'

'No, you didn't. I have them here,' the young girl replied. 'Really, Pru, anyone with a less appropriate name than yours would be difficult to find!'

Prudence grinned ruefully at her.

'Dear Netta! Even at twelve you are far more reliable than I at nineteen.

What a comfort you must be to Aunt Lavinia,' she added as she started to walk on.

'I'm not sure I am,' Netta said thoughtfully. 'When I remind her about things such as asking Cook why the meat costs so much, or why we use so many candles in the kitchen, she seems to develop a headache. That's not comfortable for her. Oh, Pru, look at that pair of greys!' she added enthusiastically, pointing to two superb, high-stepping horses trotting briskly towards them, drawing a smart phaeton in which rode two elegant young men. Netta was already an accomplished rider and currently it was her dearest wish to own a pair of carriage horses.

As she spoke the driver slowed the horses to a walk, and drawing level with the girls gestured with his whip towards the houses on the near side of the square.

'That's the house she's taken, if you please!' he said in a clear voice, but his further remarks were drowned by a sharp crack and the sound of shattering glass.

One of the greys shied, and then, further startled by a small boy running directly in front of his nose, did his best to drag the phaeton round in a circle.

Grimly silent, and with an admirable display of strength and skill, the driver soon had him under control.

'Pray take the ribbons a while,' he said curtly, handing the reins and his whip to his companion, and leaped purposefully down into the road. He strode across to where two boys, aged about eight and six, the elder carrying a cricket bat, were shamefacedly surveying the broken window in front of them.

'You!' the man said peremptorily, grasping the younger boy by the shoulder. 'Haven't you the wit not to startle a horse by running straight in front of it? I'll teach you not to do it again!' he added, and twisting the boy so that the appropriate part of his anatomy presented itself, raised his other hand in readiness to deliver chastisement.

He found his wrist gripped with small but determined hands.

'No, you fiend! Leave him alone! He's still a baby!' Prudence gasped, finding that it took all her strength to restrain that avenging hand.

He looked angrily down at her, but the fury in his eyes abated as he encountered the determined look in hers, and he released the child the better to look at her, his dark eyes twinkling in amusement.

She was well worth his scrutiny. Though of small stature, barely reaching his shoulder, she was exquisitely formed, and her face was as charming as her figure. Huge eyes of gentian blue were blazing angrily at him. They were wide set in a delicate, heart-shaped face, framed by a mop of unruly dark curls. Her lips, parted now and revealing small white teeth, were full and rosy.

Before he could speak he found his

other arm grasped by even smaller hands, and found both small boys tugging furiously at him, the younger aiming desperate kicks at his legs.

'Let Pru go!' the older boy gasped, oblivious to the fact that it was Prudence who was hanging on to their attacker, not the other way round.

'Outnumbered, by George!' the man in the phaeton said with a laugh, and Prudence, realising what she was doing, flushed in acute embarrassment and stepping hastily backwards.

'James, Harry, let go,' she ordered hurriedly. 'Look, there is Mr Kennedy's butler. Go and apologise at once for breaking his window. As for you, sir,' she added with dignity, 'you should be ashamed of yourself, attacking a small child in such a vicious way.'

She turned on her heel and, amused, he watched her march away to join the two boys, now with hanging heads, standing to receive the angry recriminations of an elderly manservant. She gave no indication of how disturbed she had been by the encounter, forcing her trembling limbs to carry her steadily, and telling herself sternly that the wild pounding of her heart was due to the fury she felt at his treatment of little Harry.

'Foiled, Richard, my lad,' his friend said softly. 'Damned fine gal despite her size. That's one whose heart you won't easily break.'

He turned to mount into the phaeton and retrieve the reins.

'Is that a wager? It's a tempting one. I'm bored and the season's hardly begun.'

'A hundred pounds you cannot bring her to heel within a month.'

'Done! A further meeting must be arranged, Edward. I have a preference for spirited damsels, the more so since I made the acquaintance of my cousin. Come, let's go and break a bottle to seal our bargain.'

They drove off, unaware of Netta standing beside the phaeton and watching them with narrowed eyes.

Prudence, her colour still high, pacified the elderly butler with a promise of sending a man round at once to repair the broken window, and bore off the two chastened boys. Netta, her expression thoughtful, gathered up the packages Prudence had scattered around her when flying to Harry's rescue, and then forgotten, and followed them into the house.

Having despatched the boys to the schoolroom, they found Lady Frome reclining on a chaise longue in the drawing-room. She was entertaining two visitors, Prudence's married sister Sarah and her friend Mrs Jane Buxton.

Lavinia Frome was still a very pretty woman, in a rather faded way, but she enjoyed conspicuously frail health, and the least exertion fatigued her alarmingly. Her niece and daughter had not needed to consult together before determining to mention no word to her of what had passed in the square.

Netta made her curtsies, delivered the packages to her mother and explained that the new cards she had ordered would be ready by the following day. Then she escaped, leaving Prudence to chat with the visitors.

Sarah Barhampton was two years older than Prudence, a taller and paler version of her sister. She had made a very good marriage when only 18 to a man 15 years her senior, who was rich, doting and in daily expectation of inheriting his father's estates.

'Augustus has returned to Sussex,' Sarah was explaining to her aunt. 'His poor father is sinking rapidly, and although I did not wish to leave them he insisted that I came to town, for you know how the sight of suffering disturbs me. I made him promise to send for me if I could be of any assistance, but he told me that I must not fret, but was to go about as usual while I can. We shall have to put on our blacks very soon, I fear. Until then, however, if you are unwell, Aunt Lavinia, I can escort Prudence to parties.'

'How kind of you, my dear, but I shall make an effort to go myself. We must do our best to find a good match for her this year. Such a pity we had to postpone her coming out last season, but I really was not able to face it after both the boys and then Netta succumbing one after the other to the measles. I was worried that Prudence herself would catch it, and if she had done so right in the middle of the season that would have been disastrous.'

'I had them when I was ten, Aunt,' Prudence said mildly, but her aunt did not appear to be listening, she was too anxious to compliment Mrs Buxton on her gown, and ask where she had acquired the matching, deep-brimmed hat.

That topic exhausted, Lady Frome suddenly recalled the news given to her by an earlier visitor.

'Sarah, I almost forget to tell you. Lady Carstaires was here an hour since, and she has it on the best authority that Lord Mottesford's widow is coming to town this year, and has actually taken a house here in the square. I wonder what she is like?'

'Have you never met her?' Mrs Buxton asked. 'I thought his estates were in Devon, and as you lived there as a girl you might have met her.'

'We lived at the opposite end of the county, and although my dear parents knew him slightly I scarcely saw him. They did not like him, he was such an evil-tempered old man. My sister, Prudence's mother, who was of course much older than I am, said he used to snub people unmercifully when he was offended with them. Then he was such a recluse after his first wife died, and as that was in my first season I remember very little of him. I believe he married the second Lady Mottesford only a few months before he died. No-one knows who she is, but she is rumoured to be a horridly vulgar person.'

'I suppose she is trying to marry off her stepdaughter,' Sarah said musingly.

'Well, we need have nothing to do

with her even if she is a neighbour,' Lady Frome said comfortingly. 'What is the new Lord Mottesford like?'

'I haven't met him,' Mrs Buxton replied, 'but Mr Buxton knew him at Eton. He's thirty, and very wealthy. His father made a fortune and his mother was a great heiress, so he won't be in need of Dicky Mottesford's money.'

'He's not married, is he?'

'No, he's been in the army since he left school, and sold out when he inherited the title last year. I understand he has been living on his own estates in Worcestershire since then, but he is bound to come to town soon. What a catch for someone! My husband says he is tall and handsome as well as being rich, although he kept somewhat aloof from the other boys at Eton, apart from his own particular cronies.'

Prudence, losing interest in this paragon who sounded both arrogant and dull, began to wonder who the man in the phaeton was and whether she would encounter him again. Her cheeks burned at the notion, and at the recollection of her unmaidenly behaviour in actually clinging to his arm.

At last Sarah and Mrs Buxton rose to depart, after inviting Prudence to walk with them in the park on the following day. Lady Frome, saying in a weak voice that she was too fatigued to receive any more visitors that day and would rest until dinner, sent Prudence away. With considerable relief she was able to retreat to her bedroom.

She had been there scarcely five minutes when Netta tapped on the door.

'May I come in? Pru, did you hear what that abominable man said?' she demanded as she threw herself full length on to the bed, an action which would have scandalised her governess if that lady could have seen her.

'What do you mean?' Prudence asked, quickly rescuing the gown she had just laid on the bed, and which she had been about to trim with new ribbons.

'That man who was going to beat Harry. I thought you were splendid,' she added fervently. 'So brave and fearless.'

'I was too angry to be afraid, and in any event what was there to be afraid of? He would scarcely have beaten me!'

'No, but he laid a wager with the other man!' Netta disclosed importantly.

'A wager? What about?'

'You!'

'Netta, don't be so irritating! Tell me what they said, at once!'

'Well, the other man said that he would not be able to break your heart, and he bet a hundred pounds that he would bring you to heel in a month!' Netta related.

Prudence stared at her in horrified amazement.

'They laid a bet on that? Are you sure?'

'Of course I'm sure. I was standing right beside him when he got back to the phaeton, and I heard it all quite plainly. I wonder what he means to do? How can he break your heart when you don't even know him? And what could he mean by saying he would bring you to heel?'

'I haven't the faintest notion, apart from knowing that it is all exceedingly vulgar, and just what I should have expected of such an odious man!' Prudence said vehemently.

'You expected him to make a wager about you?' Netta demanded in astonishment.

'No, of course not! Not that, but just his behaviour in general, which is far from being gentlemanly.'

'Well, you know now, so you can avoid him,' Netta remarked complacently. 'Wasn't it a good thing I listened?'

'I won't even speak to him, even if I do see him again,' Prudence vowed.

'Good. There's another thing, though, which Biddy told me.'

'Biddy.'

'One of the housemaids. She says

that the new people next door arrived while we were out. An elderly woman with two daughters, she thought, very fashionably dressed. Perhaps you will meet them at parties.'

'Did she also know their name? Aunt Lavinia said this morning that she did not know who was coming, but the Frintons were renting the house again this year.'

'Biddy did not know, but she is friendly with the Frinton's kitchen maid, and she will tell me tomorrow.'

'You oughtn't to gossip with the servants,' Prudence said with belated caution, but Netta grinned impishly at her.

'How else can I discover what goes on?' she asked in a reasonable tone. 'Mama thinks I am too young to be told everything, and Papa isn't in the least interested in what he calls frivolity. All he cares about is boring debates in Parliament or talking with his cronies at his clubs. You know he hardly ever goes out with Mama, unless it is some special occasion which he thinks will be of use to him politically.'

Prudence considered her cousin. Netta was a sturdy, plain child, taking after her father in looks, with no promise of the ethereal although faded beauty of her mother. It was clear that at the moment she had no idea that she also took after him in other ways, with her down to earth, outspoken common sense, and lack of sensibility in her comments on other people. She would have rejected with scorn the very suggestion that she had more in common with his political activities than the social round which occupied her mother, when Lady Frome was feeling strong enough to face that.

'Shall we ride in the park before breakfast?' Prudence suggested now, and Netta agreed enthusiastically.

Long before her mother was awake, therefore, on the following morning, Netta and her cousin were cantering in an almost deserted park, attended by Woodward, an elderly groom who had taught both of them to ride. He restrained Netta when she suggested a gallop, telling her that she would be breaking one of the rules if she did, and although she pouted she obeyed.

'Do hurry up and get married, Pru,' she said with a sigh. 'Then we can go back to Horton Grange and I can gallop on the downs as much as I please.'

Prudence laughed. 'I've no intention of marrying just to please you, Miss! And I shall take my time choosing. I insist on any husband being rich and amiable as well as handsome. He must adore me and be ready to do everything I want.'

'Have you anyone in mind yet?' Netta asked with a giggle. 'I cannot say that I know anyone with all those virtues. At least you won't be tempted by him!' she added in a different, angry tone, indicating with her whip, and Prudence looked to where she pointed.

The man from yesterday was riding

towards them, mounted on a magnificent black horse. He was alone and Prudence, before she recollected herself, thought how splendid he looked in his severe, military-style coat.

She swung away down a side path before he reached them, her heart thumping uncomfortably loudly in her breast. To her intense relief he did not attempt either to follow or to greet them, and after a while she began to breathe more easily.

'Shall we go home now?' Netta asked, and Prudence, reluctant to run the risk of meeting him if they made another circuit of the park, willingly agreed.

They reached Grosvenor Square a few minutes later, and dismounted outside their door. Woodward was taking the reins of their horses, preparatory to leading them round to the mews, when the door of the house next door opened and a yapping, bustling ball of animated fluff hurled itself down the steps and began a furious attack on the heels of the horses.

It was all Woodward could do to retain his seat and hold on to the other horses, who were tugging in fruitless efforts to escape the attentions of the dog. Prudence and Netta instinctively stepped forwards to help Woodward by taking the reins, just as a young girl, weeping hysterically, threw herself into the mêlée and tried to pull the dog from under the horses' hooves.

This sudden eruption completed the chaos. Netta's mare, a spirited but nervous creature, reared, dragging Netta off balance. Prudence grabbed at the mare as Netta stumbled, fell sideways, and, as the horses were brought under control, lay frighteningly still.

2

Handing the reins to Woodward, Prudence dropped to her knees beside her cousin. She was pale but still breathing, and already a lump was developing just above and behind her ear. Oblivious to the hysterical tears of the other girl, Prudence looked round for help and saw Tanner, her aunt's butler, coming hurriedly towards her followed by two footmen.

'Tanner, thank Heavens! Carry Miss Netta into the morning-room, and send for Doctor Baron. She was kicked, I think. Woodward, there's no more you can do, take the horses round to the stables.'

She rose to her feet, suddenly noticing that she was trembling violently, and took a deep breath to steady her nerves. As she began to follow the footman who was carrying Netta's limp form her hand was seized and she looked round, startled, to find a pretty, dark-haired girl a couple of years younger than herself, with tear stains on her cheeks and her hair in disarray, opening and closing her mouth wordlessly.

'What is it?' she asked, bewildered, and the girl burst into a flood of tears, incapable of speech.

Then Prudence noticed the dog which had been the cause of the trouble, cowering behind the girl's skirts, and realised what the girl was trying to say.

'It was your dog?' she asked, and the girl nodded vehemently, picked the animal up and hugged it close to her, and then found her voice.

'I am so very sorry! Oh, I wouldn't have hurt her for the world! Fifi is not used to town, you see, and it is so noisy, and noise excites her. She slipped through the door before anyone could prevent it. Your sister will be all right, won't she? Oh, dear, I do hope she will not be too badly hurt. Mama will kill me if she is! Please, is there anything I can do? I do so want to make amends!'

Prudence regarded the girl, who had once more dissolved into a spate of weeping. She clearly could not be left alone in the street in such a state, and no-one from the house next door was visible.

'You had best come in with us,' she said at last, both impatient with this torrent of words, and anxious to follow Netta.

The girl, with a muffled word of thanks, followed closely on Prudence's heels as she went into the house. There she found that Miss Francis, Netta's governess, had been summoned, and was capably dealing with a pair of flustered maids, a footman who, having carried Netta indoors, did not know what else to do, and Tanner, who was hovering behind her proffering feathers and hartshorn and brandy all at once.

'Biddy, pull yourself together and fetch a bowl of cold water and some clean rags. Agnes, fetch some towels and a pillow from Miss Netta's room. Charles, you may go, I have no further use for you. No, thank you, Tanner, no brandy. Please set the other things on this small table beside me, and if you can bring Dr Baron to me as soon as he arrives? Meanwhile, I think you had better try to ensure that Lady Frome is not disturbed with the news until after we have the doctor's diagnosis. We do not wish her to suffer undue anxiety. Ah, Netta, my child, lie still. No, don't attempt to sit up. You have been hit on the head and must lie quietly until the doctor has examined you. Who is this? And what is that dog doing here!'

'Oh, I beg your pardon,' the girl said in a whisper. 'Is she going to be all right? It was all my fault! Or rather the fault of naughty Fifi here. She ran out of the house, you see, and startled the horses. My name is Charlotte Ashley. We've just come to live next door, and Fifi isn't used to town traffic. Oh, I do hope she will be all right!'

'I am sure she will. But she ought to be kept quiet. Ah, Biddy, thank you. Put the bowl here. Prudence, my dear, I think that Miss Ashley ought to go back home now. They may be puzzled at her absence. I will send for you if I need any further assistance.'

Prudence, seeing that Netta was recovering her senses, nodded and drew the still agitated and protesting Charlotte out of the room.

'I feel so very responsible!' she was gasping, and seemed inclined to dissolve once more into tears. Prudence spoke hastily to avert this.

'It was an accident, you could not help it. I think you should go home now and lie down to calm yourself.'

'But I should not have a moment peace until I knew that she was better!'

'Why don't you call later today and ask how she is?' she suggested, and Charlotte, a smile breaking over her face, nodded eagerly.

'Yes, I'll do that. Oh, I do hope that we shall be friends. What is your name?'

24

'I'm sorry. I'm Prudence Lee, and she is my cousin, Netta Frome. You have just come to town, I believe?'

'Yes, I've never been before. Mama says it is time Emily — Emma, I mean, and I found husbands,' she confided with a shy smile.

'Emma? Is she your sister?'

'No, I've no brothers or sisters, and Mama is not my real mother. She died when I was born. Papa married again two years ago, and Emily — Emma, that is, is Mama's daughter. She is much older than I am, four and twenty. Papa died a year ago,' she added wistfully, and Prudence felt a surge of sympathy for her.

'My parents died years ago,' she said briskly. 'I am fortunate to live with my aunt and uncle. Now I think you ought to go home in case anyone is wondering where you are, but do come back later when I can tell you how Netta is.'

Charlotte nodded, and with a shy smile ran down the steps and towards the next house, where she plied the knocker gently. Prudence waited to ensure that she was admitted and then, seeing Doctor Baron approaching in his barouche, waited for him and escorted him to the morning-room.

He examined Netta's head, where the lump was already the size of an egg, and then cheerfully told her that she would be as right as rain in a day or so.

'But you must take this dose and then stay in bed for today, and I will come and see you again tomorrow before you get up,' he said sternly.

Netta, unusually pale, smiled and promised to be a model patient. Charles was summoned to carry her upstairs, and Prudence went with her to administer the medicine, tuck her up in bed, and sit with her until she dropped into a doze.

By this time Lady Frome had been informed by her excited maid of the calamity, and declaring that the news had disturbed her too much for her to stir out of bed that day, was demanding Prudence's presence in order to hear how it had occurred.

'Charlotte Ashley!' she exclaimed. 'I wonder if it can be Lady Mottesford who has taken the house? Ashley is her name. Did the child mention her family?'

'She said her parents were both dead, her papa a year since, and that he married again two years ago,' Prudence said.

'It certainly sounds like them. I wonder what Lady Mottesford is like? No-one knows anything about her, where she comes from, or what family. I suppose I must call on her when I am able to get about. How tedious. Now go and see how my poor Netta is, dear Prudence. I must rest, it has been so agitating.'

Two hours later Charlotte reappeared, full of renewed apologies, to ask how Netta was. When Prudence told her that Netta was still asleep, she was clearly not reassured, and her lamentations were beginning to try Prudence's patience. It was with relief that she heard Tanner announcing that Sarah and Mrs Buxton had called, and remembered her promise to walk in the park with them.

They came up to the drawing-room and Charlotte was introduced. When the accident had been explained to them, and Prudence apologised for not being ready to walk out with them, Sarah, taking pity on Charlotte's obvious embarrassment, suggested that she joined them if her mama permitted.

Half an hour later the four ladies were sauntering in the park, the two younger ones together while the elders waved to some acquaintances and stopped to talk to others.

'Do you know many people?' Charlotte asked rather timidly.

'Not very many,' Prudence admitted ruefully. 'It's my first season, too.'

'I'm not looking forward to all the parties,' Charlotte confessed, 'but Mama says I have to find a husband this year because she will not be able to afford another season. Papa left most of his money to my cousin, the new Lord Mottesford, you know.'

'I suppose the estates were entailed,' Prudence said cheerfully.

'Oh, no. Just Trelawn Manor and a few farms, which was the original estate. Papa had a great deal more, but Mama said that he believed that his heir should have most of his fortune. He left me my portion,' she added with a slight sigh, 'and I have some money from my own mother, but I don't think it is very much.'

'Don't you know?' Prudence asked, startled at Charlotte's odd mixture of ignorance and sophistication.

Everyone knew that the season was organised mainly for girls to contract suitable marriages, but most girls did not talk so openly about the necessity of finding a husband. Yet most of them knew exactly how large their portions were, and how much inducement it could be for prospective husbands.

'Mama says it is not enough to attract a fortune hunter, or anyone important,' she replied now. 'Prudence,' she added hesitantly, 'do you believe that love always comes after marriage?'

'Why should it?' Prudence asked bluntly. 'I can imagine some matches where it does, when perhaps people have not known one another well beforehand, but not always. If you thoroughly disliked someone, for instance, I do not see how marriage to them would alter that. I should think it would increase the dislike.'

'Yes, that is what I thought, despite what Mama says,' Charlotte said with a slight sigh, and Prudence eyed her with some concern. Already she was beginning to feel a protective sympathy for Charlotte, who seemed so gentle and so unprepared for the rigours of a London season.

'Well, you are very pretty and should have no difficulty in attracting a man who will love you,' she said bracingly, and then, when Sarah dropped back to walk with Charlotte, joined Mrs Buxton and spent the time with her commenting on all the latest fashions.

The following day Prudence and her aunt returned from a visit to their dressmaker to find that Lady Mottesford had left her card.

'I must be neighbourly,' Lady Frome said with a slight sigh, 'although I cannot feel any enthusiasm yet for visiting or entertaining. Not until poor dear Netta has completely recovered.'

'Doctor Baron said she was much better and could get up tomorrow,' Prudence reminded her. 'There is no lasting harm.'

'I must invite them to our small dance next week. I will leave cards tomorrow, and perhaps I can visit during the next few days. Will you send the invitation, my dear?'

Prudence, accustomed to dealing with her aunt's correspondence, duly sent off the invitations and received Lady Mottesford's acceptance. But when Lady Frome called a couple of days later she was informed that Charlotte's mama was indisposed, and unable to leave her room, and her daughter Emma was unfortunately out.

'Oh, dear, it is most irregular, not having met her,' she sighed the evening before the dance. 'I wonder if she will come?'

'Charlotte says that she is much better and looking forward to it,' Prudence consoled her.

She was far too busy supervising all the arrangements, Lady Frome complaining that she was really too exhausted to do everything herself, to give much thought to Charlotte and her mama, and was curt even with Sarah when the latter called on her way to another party.

'Bring another man?' she asked. 'By all means, bring as many as you like. Aunt Lavinia has been complaining all week that town is still too thin of company, and that there are always too few men willing to dance, most of them preferring the card room. Like Augustus,' she added.

'Pru, that's unfair. Just because he

wouldn't dance at that ghastly local assembly at Christmas. Besides, Augustus isn't in town or I'd make him do his duty and dance with you.'

'Of course, with all this fuss I'd forgotten. I'm sorry, how is his father?'

Sarah sighed. 'It varies. Every time he rallies and we think perhaps the crisis is over, so that Augustus can leave him for a few days, he has a relapse the following day.'

She departed then and Prudence at last found time to try on her ballgown, a simple, white satin dress with a silver gauze overskirt, that her aunt's maid, a skilled needlewoman, was making some slight adjustments to.

She did not need Netta's appreciative comments to know that she looked charming the next evening. Slightly flushed with the excitement of her first real London party, her eyes sparkling and her lips moist and red, she patted the silver ribbon threaded through her curls, fastened the double row of pearls about her neck, and picked up the fan encrusted with seed pearls.

When the first guests arrived, Prudence stood beside her aunt at the top of the stairs to greet them, wondering somewhat bemusedly whether she would ever remember all the names of these strangers. There seemed very few young people of her own age, and when she saw Charlotte in the hall below she smiled brightly at her, grateful for youthful company.

Then the smile froze on her face as she saw the two women ascending the stairs, Charlotte meekly walking one step behind.

The older woman wore a gown of puce silk, deeply decolleté, and in a skimpy style which would have suited a slender girl of 18 but was a disaster as it clung to her own opulent curves. Several diamond necklaces adorned the vast expanse of her bosom.

Her hands, which she was extending towards Lady Frome, were large and red, and the massive stones in the half dozen rings she wore could not disguise the rough skin. Nor could the heavy paint hide the wrinkles on her neck and face, or her smile, which revealed several decayed teeth, disguise the deeply scored lines of discontent about her nose and mouth.

'My dear Lady Lavinia!' she exclaimed in a loud, harsh voice which caused Lady Frome to shudder and blink rapidly several times in order to regain her composure. 'How exceedingly kind of you to invite me and my gals to your little party. I am exceedingly gratified, I do assure you. Mark my words, Emma, I said, with Lady Lavinia as our friend we shall soon be on the best of terms with all the town. This is Emma, Lady Lavinia, my daughter by my first. And you know dear little Charlotte, not my own flesh and blood, more's the pity, she's my second's child. But she's a good little puss, and is a great friend of my Emma. Say how d'ye do to Lady Lavinia, Emma. And this is Sir Dudley, I presume? I've heard a great deal about you, you naughty man!' she said, tapping the speechless Sir Dudley archly on the wrist with a large fan made out of what, to Prudence's astonished gaze, seemed to be ostrich feathers.

Somehow Lady Frome uttered a faint reply, and Lady Mottesford passed on, beaming widely about her, into the drawing-room. Prudence had time to notice that Emma, dressed in white muslin with inappropriately delicate, pink and blue and lemon bows dotted all over it, had hard black eyes at variance with the youthfulness of her gown. Poor Charlotte, she thought, with such a frightful stepmother and sister.

Then when the dancing began Prudence's attention was caught by the sight of Sarah entering the room, accompanied by two men.

She stumbled, and rather breathlessly apologised to her partner.

'You're pale,' he remarked. 'Have you seen a ghost?'

'I hope not,' she replied with a laugh, and as soon as the dance ended made her way to her uncle's side.

'Who is that with Sarah?' she asked urgently.

'With Sarah? The fair one is Edward Gregory, who is one of Augustus's friends,' he replied. 'The other is Richard Ashley, the new Lord Mottesford. I wonder if he knows yet that his aunt is here?' he added with a slight laugh. 'How on earth did she persuade Lavinia to invite her? I doubt if anyone else will even notice such a vulgar creature.'

Prudence did not reply. She was wondering desperately where she could hide as Lord Mottesford who had a wager with his friend that he could break her heart, approached her with slow determination.

3

'Miss Lee, you will grant me this dance?' he stated rather than asked, and before Prudence could answer had taken her hand, tucked it under his elbow, and led her away. Her attempt to drag her hand away was foiled by his unyielding grip, and without a deplorable scene she knew that she could not, for the moment, escape him.

Lord Mottesford, outwardly oblivious to the impotent fury which overwhelmed her, was chatting unconcernedly. He talked about the people in town, the clemency of the April weather, and finally, with a wickedly-attractive smile said how delighted he was to meet her.

Fortunately for Prudence's composure, the musicians then struck up and they took their places in the set dance.

During it she desperately tried to decide what would be her best ploy. Should she announce at once that she knew of the wager or, keep silent and when he felt sure of winning his bet, disillusion him by delivering the coup de grace?

Rather to her chagrin he gave her no opportunity to reveal her decision, for immediately the dance finished he thanked her briefly, walked across with her to where Lady Frome was chatting with some old friend, and smilingly took his leave.

'That dreadful creature!' Lady Frome exclaimed when the guests had all departed, and neither her husband nor her niece had any doubts about the direction of her thoughts.

'You didn't have to dance with her even more dreadful daughter,' Sir Dudley pointed out with a faint laugh. 'I shall ask to be excused from your future parties, my love.'

'Dudley, you can't!' his love wailed shrilly.

'But if they are to be present, and everyone else pointedly ignores the wretched female, I must as host pay some attention to her,' he said patiently. 'Why the deuce did you ever invite them in the first place?'

'It was all a despicable trick to wheedle her way in,' Lady Frome replied angrily. 'They must have called when we were out on purpose, and made certain that we did not meet when I returned the call. Indisposed, indeed! They had to be sure of getting the invitation before anyone set eyes on them.'

'I think that's unlikely,' Prudence said slowly. 'Do you think she even realises how vulgar she is? If she did she would surely behave differently.'

'I doubt she knows how, but she could be sure that she would not be able to meet anyone without some trickery! Never mind, I shall refuse to see her if she calls, or notice her if I meet her outside. I will not be bamboozled into recognising her!'

'Somehow, my love, I suspect she has a stronger will than you; and a greater determination to get her own way. They'll be like vultures now, especially as they live next door. You'll not be able to avoid them.'

'It's poor Charlotte I feel sorry for,' Prudence said. 'She is rather silly, but from what I hear of her father he probably neglected her dreadfully, and she has never been taught the proper way to go on. Yet one can see she is well bred, with natural good manners, and was suffering agonies of embarrassment at their behaviour.'

'She's pretty, but in a vapid sort of way. Unless she has a fortune she is unlikely to make a good match with that harridan behind her. Pru, you are not to encourage her. I've no doubt the scheming woman is relying on forcing the poor child in here, and hoping to follow.'

'Her cousin, Lord Mottesford, ought to help introduce her to the right people,' Sir Dudley remarked. 'Pity he's not married, or his wife could take over.'

'He's not likely to be married from what Sarah said. He's worth ten thousand a year even before what goes with the title, and girls have been on the catch for him for years, whenever he's been on leave. He has a reputation as a flirt but there has never been anything serious. Don't pin your hopes on him, Pru,' her aunt added warningly.

'I won't, I think he's a detestable man!' Prudence replied, and soon afterwards took herself off to bed.

Detestable or not, she tossed and turned, unable to rid her mind of his image. He was tall, so that she had to crane her neck to look up at him. Slim of figure, he nevertheless had iron hard muscles, as she had discovered both when trying to prevent him from chastising Harry, and when he had forcibly kept her at his side.

His face was thin and intelligent, with finely-drawn eyebrows above deep-set brown eyes, prominent cheekbones and a determined chin. His face swam before her eyes however hard she closed them in her attempt to blot it from her mind.

Although weary, she was up early riding in the park with Netta. More people were in London and they saw several acquaintances also taking exercise. Mr and Mrs Buxton stopped to chat, as did several other people who had been at the party. Prudence kept a wary eye open for Lord Mottesford, telling herself that she would be able to avoid an encounter, but they were about to leave the park before she saw him.

He was alone, entering through the gate they were approaching, and riding a superb chestnut which made Netta exclaim enviously. Braced to offer a snub, Prudence felt rather deflated when, with no more than a cool nod in her direction, he urged his mount into a canter and went swiftly past them.

Her frustration increased later in the day. She and her aunt were entertaining callers and, happening to be sitting with another young lady near one of the long windows in the drawing-room, Prudence looked down into the square and saw Lord Mottesford, driving a sporting-looking curricle, moving away from the house in the direction of Bond Street.

As soon as she could she went to inspect the cards left in the hall. Yes, he had duly left a card, but she was at a loss to know why he had not paid her a visit. Less worldly wise than he, she did not realise his method, arousing her interest and then appearing cool, in a deliberate design to confuse her and throw her off balance. Nor had she considered that the day after a party, when many guests would be paying duty calls, would scarcely be the best time to secure her undivided attention.

To Lady Frome's relief the deplorable Lady Mottesford and her daughter merely left cards, even though she scathingly condemned them as too large, over lavishly engraved, and in extremely vulgar taste. Her relief was, however, premature, for early on the following day Tanner, his face wooden with disapproval, announced Lady Mottesford, Miss Potter, Miss Ashley, and Mr Hubert Clutterbuck.

The man who accompanied them was no gentleman according to Lady Frome.

'He smelled of the shop! He had greasy hair, and greasy manners, and I would not have been surprised to find his hands greasy, too! Instead they were soft and hot. And his clothes! He could not have been above five and twenty, but I swear he wore corsets, his waist was so tightly pinched in. And lace on his cravat! As for his waistcoat, ugh! I've never seen anything so horrible!'

'My dear Lady Lavinia,' Lady Mottesford had gushed. 'I had to come and tell you how very much we all enjoyed your delightful party. Both my little girls were enraptured, weren't you, Emily — Emma, that is? I really must remember to stop using your nursery name now that you are out! Oh, and I do so hope you don't mind me bringing my nephew with me. Hubert did so want to meet you.

'The main purpose of my visit, dear Lady Lavinia, was to ask you and your dear husband, and Miss Prudence, of course, to dine with us tomorrow night. Do say you'll come, Charlotte and Emma are so looking forward to it.'

'I'm afraid we already have an engagement tomorrow,' Lady Frome said hastily, but her visitor was not to be thwarted.

'Of course, popular people like you are bound to be in great demand. Unlike strangers to town such as we are. Well, what is the first night you are free?'

'So what could I do? I could scarcely claim that we were going out every night,' Lady Frome explained to an incensed Sir Dudley. 'She would doubtless have watched for us from behind the curtains, and I refuse to be forced into going out when I don't want to, just to avoid the wretched woman. I accepted, we'll get it over with as speedily as possible, and then hope that in future I can avoid her. Tanner has orders to refuse me whenever possible.'

'If you think Tanner can protect you I fear you are greatly mistaken. She has her claws in you and will not let go. Could you give her a set down she would understand? Or could you snub the girl, Charlotte?' he asked Prudence.

She shook her head reluctantly.

'I feel so sorry for her. She was so mortified by the woman's behaviour, I could not be horrid to her. Besides, we had an opportunity to talk for a while, and she told me that her mama is planning to marry her to the frightful Hubert. If she receives no better offer she will have to accept. I believe she has virtually no money of her own.'

'But old Dicky Mottesford was rolling! And he was a miser, no spendthrift to fritter away his fortune. Do you mean that he didn't leave the child provided for?'

'She said she had some money of her mother's, but very little. It appears that her father left almost everything, even what was not entailed, to the new Lord Mottesford,' Prudence explained.

'Who needs it less than most men! I suppose she hopes to catch a husband for her own daughter. That will task her powers of persuasion!'

'She cannot be ill provided for if she can afford to hire a house in the square,' Lady Frome said thoughtfully. 'And those jewels, gaudy though they are, are real. Oh, bother the woman! We shall have to go to her wretched dinner party, but I have no intention of wasting all my time talking about her. I shall treat it like going to the dentist, unavoidable and to be forgotten about both before and afterwards!'

Rather guiltily Prudence decided not to mention that, sorry as she had been for Charlotte, she had invited the girl to walk in the park on the following day. She was beginning to like her, despite her timidity, and the very idea of her being forced to wed the deplorable Mr Clutterbuck was enough to make Prudence determined to do her utmost to prevent it. The only way was to introduce Charlotte into society in the hope that some more eligible man would be attracted to her, and not be deterred by her frightful stepmother and comparative lack of fortune.

She was seated in the drawing-room the following day, weaving these plans, when Tanner announced Lord Mottesford.

'Lady Frome, I came to thank you for a delightful party, and to beg you to permit Miss Lee to give me the pleasure of her company driving in the park,' he said with a smile.

Instantly determining that she would play him at his own game, she agreed, and after donning a charming blue pelisse the colour of which exactly matched her eyes, and a neat bonnet in a darker shade, she allowed him to hand her up into his curricle. He dismissed his groom and soon they were bowling along the carriageway in the park.

Prudence was reminded that it would be helpful to Charlotte if her cousin were to take her under his wing, and with that in view she related how they had met.

'Poor Charlotte, she was so distressed, and it was not her fault at all. She was a sweet girl, don't you think?'

'I really have no opinion, Miss Lee, nor do I intend to form one. I mean to do my utmost to avoid that scheming woman my poor uncle married, and her entire ménage.'

'But she — Charlotte, that is, is your cousin!'

'If she chooses to associate with people of that order that is her affair. I do not.'

'I doubt if she has any choice!' Prudence retorted heatedly. 'I understand that her father made his wife her guardian, so she has no alternative but to live with her. And how is she to meet suitable men in that household? Even if she had a huge fortune the connection would do her harm.'

'Her fortune? What do you know of that?' he asked sharply.

'Only what Charlotte herself has said. She told me she did not know how much it was, only that it was small, a little from her mother and almost nothing from her father. And I suppose that if Lady Mottesford was left very little she will wish to give her own daughter enough to marry on, and may not be able to spare any for Charlotte.'

'I see,' he responded slowly. 'Have you met the obnoxious Hubert yet?'

'Yes. They brought him to call. Charlotte is afraid she will be made to marry him, so it is even more important to put her in the way of meeting more suitable men.'

'Why do you suppose he is wanting to marry her? That sort of creature is out for all he can get, and would hardly be likely to pursue a girl with no fortune.'

'What he might consider a reasonable

fortune could be different from your own estimates,' Prudence pointed out. 'I was not told whether he worked for a living, and what his own circumstances are, but to many such as he even a few hundred a year would be affluence they could never have expected.'

'Possibly. I believe his father is a tailor, but not one of the most esteemed.'

'Not if he made the coat Mr Clutterbuck was wearing when he called!' Prudence said with a gurgle of laughter. 'Aunt Lavinia is convinced he wore corsets, he was so nipped in at the waist!'

'That would not surprise me. He has ambitions to be a dandy, I suspect, but neither the figure nor talent to achieve it.'

'Well, I shall make a point of introducing Charlotte to my friends, even if you mean to abandon her,' Prudence said with sudden determina-tion. 'I cannot endure to think of her with no alternative but to marry him! A tailor's son! Was he ever apprenticed in the trade himself?'

'I have no idea. Probably he started life as a footman, expecting to profit by his aunt's recommendation, until she rose in the world. He has that obsequious air some of the more incapable fellows adopt.'

'What was his aunt?' Prudence asked, her avid curiosity overcoming her discretion and sense of what was proper.

'Didn't you know? No, I suppose she would not have wished it known, and has probably enforced Charlotte's silence by all sorts of dire threats. My uncle, you see, was a miserly curmudgeon. None of his relatives would visit him, for they did not relish being ordered out of the house at a moment's notice if they offended him, or disregarded some notion of penny pinching he had acquired, such as having only one candle in each bedroom, and that a tallow one, and being expected to douse it five minutes after retiring!'

'How dreadful!' Prudence commented, startled at learning this about Charlotte's father.

'He could keep only those servants too old to leave, and more often than not Charlotte was without a governess. Then Mrs Potter arrived. She was the cook first of all, then when his housekeeper left he said that she could do both jobs. As she had some learning, being able to read and write, and cast accounts, she offered to teach Charlotte until she could be said to be old enough to do without a governess. That was three years ago, and my uncle must have thought he had found the solution to all his problems. He soon realised that if he married her he would not only save her salary, but she would be unable to leave him, and she was very willing to acquire a title. My uncle did not discover about Emily's existence until after the knot was tied, when she was brought from some relative and joined the family.'

'Emily. She is called Emma now,'

Prudence said slowly.

'No doubt she considers Emily too plebian a name,' he said. 'But I am bored with my relatives. Tell me about yourself. You are a far more delightful topic of conversation!'

4

Prudence returned from that drive more determined than ever that Charlotte should be given every opportunity to escape from her dreadful stepmother.

'If that unfeeling cousin refuses to help I must do it myself,' she declared to Netta. 'Although I intend to do my utmost to force him to acknowledge his responsibilities.'

'He isn't her guardian,' Netta pointed out prosaically, 'so why should he be concerned?'

'He inherited what should by rights have been her fortune,' Prudence explained heatedly. 'The very least he could do would be to ensure that she makes a suitable marriage. As well as introducing Charlotte to all my friends and taking her about with me as much as possible, I shall contrive to throw her into Lord Mottesford's way and force her on to his notice whether he wants it or not.'

'That could be difficult,' Netta said slowly.

'Why should it? He has made it plain that he will call here, for he invited me to drive again tomorrow.'

'Oh, Pru! Charlotte cannot be dragged along with you then.'

'No, but she could be here when he calls for me.'

'Then you ought not to desert her. Besides, he might not leave his horses to come into the house. Charlotte can hardly wait about on the doorstep until he arrives. She wouldn't agree, for one thing, because she told me she is scared of him.'

'When did you see her?'

'While you were out. I was with James and Harry in the square gardens, and she was taking that wretched Fifi for a walk. Not that the ghastly animal can walk far, she had to carry it back home. Why can't she have a real dog, like Bella?'

'Bella's a hunting dog, you could not have her in town. But that's beside the point. We can ride and walk in the park, where we are bound to meet lots of people.'

'She doesn't ride,' Netta informed her, her voice full of astonished contempt.

'Not ride? Not at all?' Prudence exclaimed.

'No, it's very poor-spirited of her. She says that she was thrown when she began and now if she has to travel by horseback she goes by pillion.'

'But everyone gets thrown when learning!'

'That's what I said, but it's too late now, she won't try again. So you can't ride with her.'

'Never mind,' Prudence said, recovering. 'We'll walk, which is probably better for meeting lots of people and chatting to them.'

'But you'd have to rely on accidental

meetings with Lord Mottesford in the park.'

'I could contrive, when he is with me, that Charlotte is there, too. Walking in the park when he drives me, for example.'

'Who with? You don't want the dreadful Emma with her, that would prevent Lord Mottesford from even acknowledging her. And I can't, Miss Francis is already complaining that I don't spend enough time in the schoolroom. Papa has insisted that I must spend every morning there, and have horrid piano and dancing lessons as well as doing needlework every afternoon.'

'Aunt Lavinia would invite her here when Lord Mottesford is expected, or to go with us to the Opera, surely.'

'It would be difficult without inviting Emma, too, and she won't do that. And as an unmarried girl you would be considered dreadfully fast if you your-self gave him such invitations.'

Prudence remained deep in thought

for a few moments, then smiled gleefully.

'I know, I'll make Sarah do it! She is always entertaining, even though Augustus is not in town. And so is Mrs Buxton. If Sarah asks her she will help, too. And Aunt Lavinia will do it occasionally, so between us we'll contrive lots of meetings so that the wretched man feels guilty, and Charlotte will meet lots of other men, too!'

'Will Sarah do it?'

'Of course,' Prudence replied confidently. 'I've always been able to make Sarah do what I wanted, even though she is older than I am. And if I hint to her that Lord Mottesford is interested in me she'll be contriving occasions to throw us together. Ever since she married Augustus she has considered herself an expert on marriage, and I know she has a list of dozens of men she thinks might make me suitable husbands.'

'All at once?' Netta asked, giggling.

'Don't be a pea-goose! Good, that's

settled. I'll go round to Mount Street now and talk to Sarah.'

'And I'd better do some more of that hemming before Miss Francis discovers that I am down here with you. How I hate plain sewing!'

Sarah was easily persuaded to fall in with her sister's schemes, their objectives carefully adapted to engage her sympathy. She heartily approved Prudence's wish to detach the gentle Charlotte from her obnoxious family, and robustly declared that she would brave Lady Mottesford's displeasure by excluding her and Emma as much as she could from the invitations issued to Charlotte.

'I shall have to ask them occasionally,' she sighed. 'But if you and Charlotte can give me advance warning of when her stepmother and sister are otherwise engaged, I can arrange small parties which she would not think worth attending.'

'Good. Netta can help there. She's always gossiping with the servants. She can discover through Biddy, who has started walking out with one of Lady Mottesford's footmen, what her engagements are.'

Sarah, always an indefatigable hostess, was delighted with her new task, and soon devised a host of entertainments suitable for Charlotte but which she was sure would not attract Lady Mottesford. It was easy for her to meet Lord Mottesford, and invite him to her parties. Prudence meanwhile soon discovered that he rode regularly in the park during the early mornings and, sacrificing her own preference for riding, to Netta's disgust, persuaded Charlotte to walk there with her.

It proved easy to contrive meetings, and soon Lord Mottesford began to feel that he would never find Prudence alone. Only when he could induce her to drive with him was he certain of having her to himself.

True to her first design of encouraging him to think that he was on the way to win his wager, she deliberately allowed herself to appear pleased at his attentions, and occasionally exhibited signs of flustered agitation which Netta viewed with all the contempt of her 12 years.

'You blushed, and fluttered your eyelids at him in an utterly revolting way,' that damsel accused one morning when, Charlotte being unable to accompany Prudence on her normal walk, she had ridden out with Netta instead.

'I did not!' Prudence responded vehemently, and then spoiled the effect by adding that she had merely been playing her part in deceiving him with regard to the wager.

'That wasn't how it looked to me,' Netta said with a sniff. 'You'd best be careful you don't allow him to win it!'

'Edward Gregory seems very taken with Charlotte,' Prudence said after a slight pause.

'The man who made the wager?'

'Yes. He lives near to Lord Mottes-ford in Worcestershire, and they were at school together. He was talking to her for hours last night.'

'Does she like him?'

'It seemed so, from the way she was smiling up at him, with rather a foolish look on her face and as if she couldn't take her eyes from him.'

'Like you with Lord Mottesford.'

'Of course it was nothing of the kind! You are an abominable child!' Prudence raged, forgetting the rules of the park and urging her mare into a gallop. 'I won't tell you any more if you make such unfounded remarks,' she added when, her hair windblown, she had reined in at the far end of the park and allowed Netta to come up to her.

'You need me for military intelligence,' Netta replied, unconcerned. 'When you marry him will you persuade him to allow me to drive his greys? He said no when I asked him.'

'I have no intention of marrying a man who thinks that he can bring me to heel, merely in order to win a despicable wager, and in any case you know perfectly well that he has no idea of marrying me, it's all that wretched wager!' Prudence retorted, and rode home wrapped in an air of offended dignity which disturbed her young cousin not at all. Netta, indeed, seemed to be finding considerable amusement in the situation.

Perhaps because she was already ruffled, and because he himself introduced the topic, Prudence attacked Lord Mottesford directly later in the day when, dressed in a new gown of sprigged muslin and an enchanting bonnet which partly masked her face, she was driving with him.

'It is a rare pleasure to have you to myself,' he remarked as they turned into the park. 'I find the constant attendance of my poor little dab of a cousin most frustrating. What on earth do you find to say to her? She never has more than a frightened word for me.'

'Is that surprising?' Prudence demanded hotly. 'The child is terrified of you, and no wonder after her papa left almost everything to you. She has lost her home, the only one she ever knew, and is now largely dependent on her frightful stepmother. Is it surprising that she feels some resentment towards you, and fear?'

'Is that what she told you? I understood that she had her mother's fortune secured on her.'

'But that is minute, and Lady Mottesford was left to administer it until she marries or is thirty! I ask you, thirty! It's positively gothic! She tells me that the wretched woman is growing more insistent that she accepts that worm Clutterbuck, too. You really owe it to her to introduce her to your friends, to give her a better opportunity of attracting more suitable men, and I really do think that as you inherited all her papa's money you ought to provide her with a settlement, too,' Prudence continued, her annoyance carrying her beyond the bounds of civility.

Lord Mottesford had halted the phaeton and was regarding her with uplifted brows. Prudence blushed to the roots of her hair as she realised how her indiscreet tongue had betrayed her into such impoliteness.

'Oh, I do beg your pardon!' she gasped. 'I know that it is none of my business, but I feel so sorry for her! Pray forgive me.'

He smiled, but distantly.

'Of course, Miss Lee. Your concern does you credit,' he said smoothly. 'Is that why you persist in burdening yourself with her company so often?'

'Yes, for if you won't — that is, someone must make a push to introduce her into proper society!'

'I cannot understand about this fellow Clutterbuck. If Lady Mottesford is so keen to marry Charlotte off to him, why does she permit the chit to spend so much time with you and your sister, in case what you hope and she must fear will happen?'

Prudence chuckled, forgetting the coolness that had arisen between them.

'She dare not offend Aunt Lavinia or

Sarah, while there is the slightest chance that they will include her and Emma in their invitations. She is determined to find Emma a rich husband, she says, although even she must see that the likelihood of that is exceedingly remote.' Suddenly she giggled. 'Sarah was magnificent. Without actually promising, she hinted that as she was acquainted with Mrs Burrell she might be able to obtain vouchers for Almack's. Of course Lady Mottesford immediately concluded that Sarah was promising to obtain them for her, and she will be as agreeable as she knows how to be while there is that hope.'

He laughed. 'Unprincipled! But there isn't the slightest hope of her receiving vouchers, nor Charlotte, of course, as she must know.'

'She is too puffed up to accept that. Did you know that she actually wrote to Sally Jersey and asked for them?'

'No! What on earth did Sally say?'

'I don't know, but Charlotte said that

when her letter was returned with a note enclosed, she went as red as a turkey cock and later the same day both the cook and her own maid gave in their notices and actually left without working out their months.'

He chuckled. 'That is a note I would dearly love to read. I wonder if Sally would tell me what she said? What a set down it must have been!'

'Oh, pray tell me if she confides in you!' Prudence urged impetuously, and he smiled down at her with a warm look in his eyes which caused her to blush rosily.

'On one condition,' he promised, and, suddenly wary, Prudence eyed him with suspicion.

'What is it?' she asked at last.

'That you will join a party I am organising to Vauxhall Gardens,' he replied. 'And to satisfy you I will even invite my cousin. Will your sister come, too?'

In the end a dozen young people went by barge to the famous pleasure ground, where they danced in the Pavilion, admired the various temples in different styles, ate a delicious supper in one of the booths, and walked through the dimly-lighted paths where it was easy to lose one's way.

Prudence was gratified to note that Lord Mottesford paid a great deal of attention to his cousin, and he was clearly successful at putting her at ease, for she was soon chatting to him uninhibitedly. She preened herself on having brought him to realise his responsibilities, and therefore smiled on him with more than usual friendliness.

Edward Gregory was also paying Charlotte great attention, and Sarah took an opportunity, under cover of the strains of the orchestra, to whisper her hopes to Prudence.

'He is enchanted, you can see that,' she gloated. 'What a triumph if he offers for her.'

'Do you think he might? She has not confided much in me, but I suspect that she is losing her heart to him,'

Prudence replied slowly.

'He has a tolerable fortune, not as great as Lord Mottesford's, to be sure,' Sarah replied, 'but enough so that he does not need to dangle for a rich wife. Her lack of fortune will not deter him. She's a sweet child, even if she's not very clever, and after the dreadful childhood she has had I would like her to be happy.'

'And I cannot wait to put a spoke into that detestable Hubert's wheel!' Prudence added. 'He was paying me the most oily compliments yesterday when I was walking with Charlotte. We met him in the park.'

'Is he often there?'

'Yes, several times during the past week. I have the horrid suspicion that he knows we go regularly and follows us,' Prudence said despondently.

'Lady Mottesford has probably told him, so that he can spy on what you do.'

'What puzzles me is that he doesn't make any attempt to ingratiate himself

with Charlotte. He's far more concerned about making an impression on
me. If only he knew how different it is
from what he would wish!'

'Perhaps he doesn't wish to marry
her after all,' Sarah suggested.

'I cannot believe that, for Emma
makes it plain that she regards it as
certain. Did you see her ogling old
Lord Finchampton last night?' she
asked with a sudden giggle.

'Wasn't she making a spectacle of
herself! He must be almost sixty. And
how did that woman manage to obtain
an invitation? She is beginning to force
her way in everywhere.'

'People cannot always bring themselves to snub her effectively, and she is
so determined to ignore hints.'

'I feel guilty,' Prudence confessed. 'If
I hadn't met Charlotte and persuaded
Aunt Lavinia to invite her to her dance
she might not have gained so much
acceptance.'

'It's too late to be concerned about
that, and in any event we are trying to

help Charlotte. If we can find her a good match that will outweigh the disadvantages of having to recognise Lady Mottesford,' Sarah consoled her. 'Oh, do look, there is Sir Tarquin Maltravers in that dreadful striped waistcoat. He is worse than any woman for gossip, so don't ever offend him!'

Prudence was even more comforted when she observed Charlotte and Mr Gregory vanishing along one of the less brightly illuminated walks and, her thoughts busy with them, did not realise that Lord Mottesford had drawn her aside into a dark, unfrequented path.

Lord Mottesford had also, it seemed, noticed their discreet disappearance.

'I suspect your worries about my cousin will soon be groundless,' he said softly, 'and then you will be able to pay more heed to me.'

Prudence glanced up at him in alarm. It was so dark that she could barely distinguish his features.

'I am sorry if I have been inattentive,'

she replied primly. 'Did you ask me a question that I have not heard?'

He chuckled. 'Not yet, my sweet, and when I do ask it I shall make very sure that you are paying me proper attention!'

Before she could answer he halted, turned her round so that she was facing him, and took her shoulders in his hands.

'You must have realised how much I have wanted to do this!' he said in a low, husky voice, and before she could move he had slipped his arms tightly about her and pulled her close to him, his lips, softer and warmer than she had imagined, closing on hers.

5

A moment of sheer astonishment was succeeded by several moments during which Prudence relaxed, blissfully content, as though this sensation which swept through her was something she had been waiting for all her life. Then she recalled the wager and was consumed by shame and anger, the one because she had for even a brief time submitted to his blandishments, the other because of his unscrupulous manner of winning his wager.

She struggled to free herself, wrenching her lips away from his, and beating her fists against his chest.

'Let me go!' she said furiously, but her voice contained a note of pleading which Lord Mottesford was quick to recognise.

'My dear, have I been too sudden?'

he asked solicitously. 'I had no wish to frighten you.'

'You did not frighten me!' Prudence retorted angrily. 'How could you behave so despicably! Take me back to Sarah at once!'

Without waiting for his reply she walked swiftly past him, and back along the paths until she came to where Sarah and some of the others sat in a booth. She knew that she was flushed, and try as she might she was unable to still the trembling which attacked her limbs, so she sat down as far back in the shadows as she could, busily fanning her burning cheeks.

Lord Mottesford had accompanied her, without attempting to speak, but as soon as she was settled he went to sit beside Sarah and began to talk easily to her.

How could he appear so unconcerned after what had happened, Prudence raged inwardly, and then rather bleakly told herself that he was no doubt accustomed to such scenes.

She recalled with renewed shame the moments when she had forgotten everything apart from the bliss of being enfolded in his arms, and the rightness of his warm soft lips against hers. She took a deep breath, vowing that never again would she be taken in by his wiles.

It was with this resolution in mind that she refused his invitation to drive out with him the following day.

'I have too many engagements, my lord,' she replied when, having spoken no further word to her for the remainder of the evening, he sat beside her in the barge which carried them back across the river, and asked her if he might call on the following morning.

Somewhat to her chagrin he merely nodded, then turned to speak to his other neighbour, and they exchanged no more words apart from cool farewells.

For several days Prudence saw no more of Lord Mottesford than the occasional glimpse across the park. He was never present at the routs and balls and receptions she attended, nor at Almacks when Lady Frome took her there for her first visit. Sarah persuaded her to walk in the park one afternoon, and regarding her with ill-concealed curiosity, asked whether he had called in Grosvenor Square. On being told that he had not she asked bluntly whether they had quarrelled.

'For he was paying you most decided attentions,' she said rather plaintively. 'What a triumph it would be if you were to catch him! He's the ideal age for you, as well as being rich and handsome!'

'Pooh, he's a flirt,' Prudence declared, 'and there is nothing whatsoever for us to quarrel about. Oh, there is Charlotte, shall we join her?'

'Not while that dreadful little man is with her!' Sarah replied with a shudder.

'Hubert Clutterbuck. At least we don't have to suffer him at all of the parties that her pushy stepmother manages to attend. Oh, Sarah, she looks dreadfully uncomfortable, as though she is hunted! Do let us join them.'

Before they could come up with Charlotte and her dandified escort, however, the pair had turned down a narrow side path, screened on both sides with dusty evergreen shrubs. Sarah hesitated, but Prudence was undaunted, convinced that Charlotte had no desire to be alone with the deplorable Hubert, and in so secluded a spot. She plunged after them down the gloomy path.

A few yards along it there was a bend, and as she neared this Prudence heard the sound of a scuffle, a sharp slap, then a cry of protest.

As she rounded the bend, with Sarah a few steps behind her, she found Charlotte, closely pinioned by his arms, struggling to evade Mr Clutterbuck's kisses.

'Charlotte!' she exclaimed, and Hubert released her so quickly that Charlotte almost fell.

'Prudence! Oh, how thankful I am to

see you!' Charlotte gasped. 'I could not get away!'

'You're safe now,' Prudence said reassuringly, 'As for you, sir, you should be ashamed to treat a girl left in your care in so dastardly a fashion!'

'You're a pair of prudes!' Hubert blustered, losing his battle to remain calm. 'Teases, both of you, asking for attention, and when a fellow accepts the invitation, you get frightened and pretend innocence.'

'That is quite enough,' Sarah intervened angrily. 'I will thank you not to insult my sister or her friend. Come, Charlotte, we will escort you back home.'

With the sisters on either side of her Charlotte went willingly, biting her lip in order to control the trembling which had attacked her.

'Don't try to talk,' Sarah advised calmly. 'Pru, isn't that Lady Jersey in the barouche? Did you hear what she said last night about Sir Roland Mortimer?'

Chatting lightly, they linked arms with Charlotte, and after a while she was able to speak calmly.

'Thank you both,' she whispered. 'What will Mama say?'

'I should hope she will be angry with the sneaking little horror!' Prudence said sharply. 'Why were you alone with him anyway? Doesn't your maid accompany you?'

Charlotte sighed. 'Mama told me she need not. You see, he wants to marry me, and she says that I must.'

'Marry Hubert?' Prudence exclaimed. 'Oh, Charlotte, you cannot!'

'I don't want to,' Charlotte confessed with a sigh. 'I did hope that — well, that someone else might offer to marry me even though I have so little fortune, but Mama says I must not think of it. She says I must be grateful that Hubert is willing to accept me without.'

'It's monstrous!' Prudence exclaimed, but bit back her query about Edward Gregory.

He had appeared to like Charlotte,

and she was certain it was Edward the girl was thinking of. Without knowing anything of his intentions, however, there did not seem much point in discussing whatever hopes Charlotte might have in that direction, as there was no encouragement she could offer. Instead, she and Sarah attempted to distract Charlotte's thoughts as they walked home with her.

'Will your mama be angry with you?' Prudence asked as they reached Grosvenor Square.

'She is out with Emma, shopping,' Charlotte replied. 'But do come in with me, I want to show you my gown for Mama's masquerade.'

'I'll tell Aunt Lavinia where you are, Pru,' Sarah offered. 'I must see her before I go home.'

Charlotte whisked Prudence up to her small bedroom on the third floor, overlooking the back of the house, and heaved a sigh of relief as she closed the door.

'What can I do?' she asked baldly,

sinking down on to the bed while Prudence sat in a small chair near to the window.

'If you are firm she can't force you to marry him,' Prudence said bracingly, although privately she considered that Charlotte was not made of sufficiently strong material to resist her formidable stepmother.

'But what else could I do? She has said that she will not continue to provide me with a home if I refuse him, and I have no-one else to go to. Oh, how I wish that Papa had not married her!'

'Isn't she your guardian?' Prudence asked, shocked at this revelation. 'She cannot throw you out into the street!'

'I — I think so, although when he was ill at the end Papa said he would make other arrangements for me. But I don't think he did, because he died the following day, and no-one from outside, like a lawyer, had been to see him for weeks beforehand. Only the doctor, and he was one of Mama's cronies.'

'And you really don't know what your fortune is?' Prudence asked. 'Have you asked her?'

'Yes, but she says girls can't understand such things, and it will be the responsibility of my husband to deal with such matters. I know that she is using the income for my dresses. She said that it would be an investment.'

Prudence once more bit back the comment that rose to her lips. Charlotte must know that compared with most girls making their come out she was poorly dressed. She would probably put that down to lack of money for finery, but the more fashion-wise Prudence was well aware that for the same amount of money she could have been more attractively garbed had her stepmother paid attention to what suited her.

Charlotte meanwhile had risen from the bed and was searching for something in the back of a drawer. She found what it was and pulled it out, turning rather shyly to show it to Prudence.

'Look, Papa gave me that, the day before he died. It's the only thing of his that I have. There was also a string of pearls that had belonged to my mother, but Mama took them, she said it was unsuitable for me to wear them.'

Prudence looked at the small and simple oblong wooden box and swallowed hard. It was not even pretty, for it had been roughly used in the past and the edges were battered. The marquetry on the lid was old, many of the intricate pieces of coloured woods missing and the velvet pad lining it was torn at one side, scuffed and stained.

What a dreadful man Charlotte's father must have been, she thought angrily. He had willed all his money either to the woman he had married in order to save himself the wages of a housekeeper, or to a man who did not need it, and left his daughter virtually penniless. Then he had given her this paltry keepsake. If she had been treated in such a despicable fashion she would have hurled the pathetic memento on to the nearest fire, she decided, and yet Charlotte appeared to treasure it greatly.

Perhaps if her father had never demonstrated much love for her, even such a paltry gesture might have meant a great deal, Prudence concluded sadly. Possibly Charlotte nourished hopes that after a lifetime of neglect her father had made a deathbed repentance. A pity it had not taken a more practical form, she fumed, but silently, because she realised that she could not shatter Charlotte's fragile links with her father.

'Show me your dress for the masquerade,' she said bracingly, changing the subject before she could be betrayed into improper comments.

Aunt Lavinia had been scathing in her comments when Lady Mottesford's invitation had arrived a few days earlier.

'Just like the dreadful woman! Instead of a proper ball to launch Charlotte, and Emma, too, I suppose, she must make it a masquerade. An excuse for romping and loose behaviour totally unsuitable for a coming out party. I've a good mind to send our excuses.'

Second thoughts, and a real fondness for Charlotte, prevented her from delivering such a snub, although on every intervening day she delivered a homily about encroaching mushrooms, and declared that nothing would persuade her to don fancy dress. Dominos and masks would have to suffice.

Prudence had been somewhat regretful at this decision, but when she saw the gown Charlotte produced she was at first heartily thankful for it.

Lady Mottesford must have found the dress in a trunk in the attics of Trelawn Manor, were her first thoughts. It was a ball gown in the style of 50 years earlier, with wide skirts and a loosely-flowing saque back. The overskirt and very low bodice were of flowered yellow brocade, edged with faded yellow lace and limp, cream-coloured bows. There was a stiff, pointed cream stomacher and an underskirt of dirty white satin, with deep flounces at the hem, and the whole was worn over a large ungainly hoop.

'Do you like it?' Charlotte asked wistfully. 'Emma has one very similar, but hers is pink.'

Prudence swallowed her instinctive retort. How could the woman, even at a masquerade, allow the girls to appear as such frights?

'Don't you think it will be difficult to manage those skirts?' she asked instead.

'It will be awkward, I suppose, especially dancing, but Mama says we shall soon get used to it. She wore such gowns when she was young.'

Not if she was a cook, Prudence thought wrathfully. A fierce determination to prevent Charlotte from wearing such a disastrous gown seized her.

'Charlotte, I've had an idea! I haven't found a costume yet, but Uncle Dudley has several books with illustrations of ancient Greek and Roman people, and from what I recall their dresses were simple tunics and cloaks. Come and look at them with me, and we will find costumes which are easy for us to make. And let us keep it as a surprise for your Mama,' she added hurriedly.

By the way Charlotte's eyes lit up Prudence knew that she had her own doubts about the gown, and they gleefully arranged that Charlotte would come later that day to talk about ideas.

Apart from distracting Charlotte's mind from the threat of marriage with Hubert Clutterbuck, and trying to bolster her courage, there was nothing Prudence could do. Back at home she tried to weave plans for discovering whether Edward Gregory's affections were engaged, but there seemed little hope of this. She had always treated him coldly, as the author of the wager with Lord Mottesford, and could scarcely change towards him in order to demand whether he loved Charlotte.

And while Lord Mottesford himself kept at a distance there seemed little hope of making any useful inquiries.

At last she decided to confide in Sarah, and urge her to try to discover what Mr Gregory's feelings were. They were both attending the opera that evening, and as they waited for it to begin Prudence signalled to Sarah, in a box opposite, that she needed to talk with her.

It was a moment later that she realised that Lord Mottesford was one of the party in Sarah's box, and during the first act she followed none of the action on stage. If he should accompany Sarah to the Fromes' box in the interval, should she make it plain that he was forgiven? Would this enable her, perhaps, to find out more?

She had not decided when the first interval began, so that when Sarah appeared, escorted by Lord Mottesford, Prudence gave him a rather uncertain smile. He raised his eyebrows fractionally as he greeted her, and she blushed furiously, and as soon as possible drew Sarah away to the back of the box where she rapidly told her all that Charlotte had revealed to her.

'Mr Gregory is her only hope, or that wretched woman will force her to marry the odious Hubert,' she concluded. 'How can we discover what he intends?'

'I'll tell Edward he has offered for her, but she is reluctant,' Sarah said after a moment's reflection. 'If he loves her that will spur him into making his own declaration. If he does not there is nothing we can do.'

Prudence sighed with relief.

'Is it so easy?' she asked. 'I am certain he loves her, he looks at her so tenderly. Is he going to their masquerade?'

'Yes, for he was wondering what to wear when I saw him yesterday.'

'That woman!' Prudence exclaimed. 'She was going to make Charlotte wear some frightful outmoded dress with hoops, and even make her powder her hair! We spent the afternoon deciding on something else, and decided that the quickest thing to make was a Roman toga. Why don't you suggest that Edward wears Roman costume as well?'

Sarah just had time to agree before it was time to return to their own box for the second act. As he rose to depart Lord Mottesford paused beside Prudence.

'May I come back?' he asked quietly. 'We can walk outside and talk for a few moments, if you will.'

Without waiting for her reply he nodded and left, and she was thrown into confusion so that she saw no more of the second act than she had of the first.

6

'I came to apologise for the other night,' Lord Mottesford said abruptly, when Prudence, incapable of finding an excuse to refuse to walk with him in the corridor outside the boxes, had meekly accompanied him. 'Will you forgive me, and let us go on as before?'

Prudence glanced up at him through her lashes. He was looking at her so warmly that she had to remind herself forcefully that it was all pretence, he cared only for the wager, and so had to resume his pursuit of her.

'I — it was — I don't know,' she whispered, heartily despising herself for such weak vacillation, but totally incapable of responding as she knew she ought, with anger and contempt of his tactics.

'My only excuse is that you are so enchanting,' he said in a low, caressing voice. 'But if you prefer it, I will engage not to mention that, not even to pay you normal compliments until you give me leave. Will you drive with me in the morning so that I can demonstrate the firmness of my resolution?'

She could not refuse. Despite her knowledge of his perfidy Prudence suddenly realised how empty the last few days had been without his company. Whatever the danger to her own contentment she wanted to be with him, to talk and laugh in the way that had become so natural between them.

'Very well, my lord,' she said quietly, and after a brief word of thanks he began to talk of the opera, permitting her time to recover from the trembling which again attacked her before he returned with her to the Fromes' box.

That night she found it difficult to sleep. It was foolish of her to encourage him when she knew the truth, she told herself firmly, and replied that it would soon be over, for when he lost the wager he would have no need to seek out her company. She would have only a few more chances to be with him, and surely making the most of them would not hurt any more than the knowledge of how he was treating her hurt at the moment.

Did she want him to win the wager, her uncomfortable inner voice demanded, and she realised with horror that if she continued to behave as she was doing, he stood to do just that.

With that in mind she was cool and distant when he called for her, although she had not been able to deny herself the pleasure of wearing a smart new gown of rose pink muslin, with a matching hat that framed her face in a delightfully saucy manner. He did not refer to Vauxhall, or say a word which could possibly offend, but as they parted he looked deep into her eyes and said that he much looked forward to seeing her that evening at Lady Carstaires' ball.

Lady Mottesford and Emma were emerging from their house as Prudence went in, and she heard Lady Mottesford hailing Lord Mottesford loudly.

'My dear Richard, how delightful to see you!' she called, but as Tanner was waiting to close the door Prudence heard no more.

'I am rather surprised that Lady Mottesford is on such familiar terms with him,' she said a few minutes later to Netta, whom she discovered waiting for her in her bedroom.

'It's just her,' Netta said with a shrug. 'Look how she insists on calling my mother Lady Lavinia instead of Lady Frome. She is trying to demonstrate that she is on familiar terms with people when she isn't. It's all pretence.'

Prudence was unconvinced. 'I cannot imagine who cares,' she said pettishly. 'Why are you not in the schoolroom?'

'Miss Francis has taken the boys out to some ghastly museum. I said I would help you make your Roman toga,' she explained, indicating the unfolded garment which reposed on Prudence's bed beside her. 'That's far more useful plain sewing than hemming sheets!'

'You have done a great deal, I can see!' Prudence said with an attempt at a laugh.

'Well, that was only an excuse. Biddy says that the servants next door have heard that Charlotte is to be betrothed soon. Did you know?'

'Is it definite? She told me the dreadful Hubert had offered for her, although she did not want to accept. Her stepmother insists that she does, however.'

'She ought to run away.'

'Don't be silly, where on earth could she go?'

'She could be a chamber maid, or a governess. I don't know, but anything must be better than marrying that ridiculous man.'

'Perhaps there will be some way out,' Prudence said slowly. She did not want to reveal to Netta her hopes that Edward Gregory might offer for Charlotte, in case nothing came of it.

'What puzzles me is why the

wretched woman went to all the expense of a London season when Hubert was there all the time, ready and willing to marry Charlotte. If they wanted that it was risky introducing her to other men. Biddy says that she, Lady Mottesford, is always complaining about the waste of money, and makes the cook account to her for every penny spent. And according to her the refreshments she is planning for their masquerade are not at all what people will expect, and only enough to feed half the people coming!'

'Thanks, I'll have a good dinner before I go,' Prudence said. 'But I imagine she hopes to find Emma a husband, too, and the season is really for her. Charlotte is here simply to try to make them acceptable to the ton. At least she is of good birth, and people will put up with her stepmother for her sake, as we do.'

'Who in the world would want to marry Emma?' Netta demanded, scandalised. 'Apart from being the daughter of a cook, and goodness knows who her father was, she's not even pretty, and she must be at least five and twenty! And so far as we know she has no fortune either.'

'She might catch a widower as mean as Charlotte's father,' Prudence suggested with a faint laugh. 'Now I must try to finish this gown, for I have to help Charlotte with hers, she cannot take it home to work on.'

'What will her stepmother say when she doesn't wear that other terrible one?' Netta asked, picking up the garment and beginning to work on it.

'There isn't much she can say at the time,' Prudence replied hopefully, but without real conviction. She was determined to carry out her plan, as was Charlotte, but she had little confidence that Lady Mottesford would not make a fuss, probably in public, when she discovered the change.

'How is Lord Mottesford behaving?' Netta asked a few minutes later. 'He has only a couple of days left before the month is up.'

'Does he?' Prudence asked, startled. She had not kept track of the days. 'I don't think he can claim to have won,' she replied thoughtfully, torn between satisfaction at having foiled him, and a bleak feeling that there would soon be no reason for him to seek her company.

She could not find an excuse for not wearing her latest ball gown, in shimmering pale-blue silk, with a gauzy floating overskirt of silver net. She was wary, however, when Lord Mottesford sought her out at the ball, and solicited her hand both for the first cotillion, then the supper dance, a waltz.

The cotillion gave them little chance for conversation, and Prudence relaxed. When she saw Edward leading Charlotte into another set, smiling fondly down at her, she smiled herself. It seemed that he was interested, and if Sarah had managed to tell him of Hubert's offer he must act soon.

'There is to be a balloon ascent in the park tomorrow,' Lord Mottesford told her as he escorted her back to where Lady Frome sat with a group of friends. 'Will you come with me to see it?'

'Oh, I have never seen a balloon,' Prudence said, her eyes lighting up eagerly. 'Yes, indeed, I would love to!' she accepted, before she realised that she had not intended to be more than icily polite.

'Good, then I will arrange it. Farewell until the waltz,' he added in a low tone.

Prudence bit her lip in annoyance. She had given him encouragement at just the wrong moment. She would betray herself if he showed too much admiration, and the waltz was not the sort of dance she would have wished to partner him in, it was far too disturbing with a man's arm holding one so daringly.

She need not have been concerned. He was not in the least amorous as he guided her round the ballroom, holding her impersonally and chatting about innocuous topics so that she gradually gave herself up to the swaying rhythm of the music, and the thrills of spinning round so gracefully.

'You dance excellently,' he complimented her after they had settled themselves at a small table in the supper room. 'I hope I can look forward to many more waltzes with you.'

She paused about to bite into a lobster patty, and regarded him with a slight frown. Was he being honest, did he intend to seek her out once the month of the wager was up, or was this just one more ploy during the last few days by which he hoped to win it?

It was impossible to tell, and she found herself that night, restless and unable to sleep, counting off the days since they had met and reliving the occasions when, despite it all, she had been so happy in his company. She finally fell asleep with the realisation that there were two days to go. Two more days when she dared not reveal how she felt towards him, both because she was determined he would not win the wager, and to safeguard herself against hurt when it became plain that he cared nothing for her.

The following day he was as imperturbable as ever, while Prudence's mood veered between cool determination to snub him, and uncontrollable excitement at this, her first sight of a balloon ascent.

'Where will they take it?' she asked as they drove with a throng of other carriages towards the enclosure where the men were getting the balloon ready.

'That depends on the wind. It's quite fresh today, from the south west, so they will be blown towards Essex, probably to the east of Barnet.'

'So far?'

'It could be much farther. I am no expert, but I believe it depends on how high they can get at first.'

'How does it work?'

'The balloon is filled with a gas such as hydrogen which is much lighter than air, and so it rises. They have ballast in the basket, and throw it out to help the balloon rise.'

'And to come down? Can they control it? It must be terribly dangerous!'

'I'm not certain how they do that, but it is possible, probably by letting the gas escape. Some flights are made with hot air, which is lighter than cold air, and when they let out the fire beneath the air inside the balloon cools down.'

'But they have to go where the wind takes them. Netta says that it is a fashion which people will soon lose interest in, for it has no possible use. Oh, look, there it is!'

Lord Mottesford was able to find a place for his phaeton in the front row of vehicles, filled with excited spectators, and for an hour Prudence forgot all her problems as, fascinated, she watched the preparations in the enclosure about the balloon, and finally, to the cheers of the spectators, the ascent itself.

They turned to watch the balloon, with the two intrepid men in the small basket below it, float away in a north easterly direction, and Prudence sighed with immense satisfaction.

'I'd like to go up in one,' she said dreamily. 'Just imagine what it must be like to see the houses and fields and woods spread out miles beneath. Much better than looking down from a hillside. Have you ever been up a really high mountain?' she asked suddenly, turning to Lord Mottesford.

'Yes, in Spain. And I plan to visit Italy when we have defeated Napoleon, which should be within a year, at most. I shall go by way of Switzerland and the Alps.'

Prudence sighed slightly. 'I envy you,' she said slowly. 'I've always longed to travel, but Aunt Lavinia hates it, and we rarely go anywhere except between Horton Grange and London.'

He did not reply, and glancing up at him she saw that he was looking intently across the enclosure to where the carriages on the far side were now visible.

'I did not know that Edward planned to be here,' he said after a slight pause.

Prudence could now see Edward, who was mounted on a large bay horse. He was beside a barouche which contained Lady Mottesford, Emma, Charlotte and Hubert. Even at this distance Prudence could sense Hubert's antagonism towards Edward, while she could see the timid glances Charlotte cast up at him. She was very much afraid that the determined smile on Lady Mottesford's face concealed a mood of fury, and wondered what had happened to cause it.

'He seems much taken with your cousin,' Prudence ventured, and he looked down at her in amusement.

'Matchmaking?' he asked teasingly, and she flushed.

'It would be better for her than that worm Hubert!' she snapped. 'Even with no money Mr Gregory would be fortunate to win so sweet and gentle a creature!'

'Instead of a termagent,' he said softly, but before she could respond he had seen a gap in the crowd and unerringly guided his phaeton into it. By the time he had cleared it Prudence had recalled the inadvisability of engaging in word battles with him, and she replied in monosyllables during the short drive back to Grosvenor Square.

'Thank you for taking me to see the ascent,' she said, holding out her hand as she prepared to descend from the phaeton, but to her surprise he gave the reins to his groom, perched up behind them, and the man drove off as he escorted her up the steps.

Tanner appeared to expect him, and Prudence, puzzled, heard the butler say that Sir Dudley was waiting for him in the library. She escaped to her bedroom, and after taking off her bonnet sat down thoughtfully, wondering what business he could possibly have with her uncle. So far as she knew they were not on especially friendly terms, for her uncle was at least 15 years older than Lord Mottesford.

She concluded that as they were both interested in politics it must be something to do with that, and picked up the Roman toga, which was almost finished, to make a start on the hem.

Five minutes later there was a tap on the door and Biddy appeared.

'If you please, Miss Prudence, Sir Dudley wishes to see you in the library,' the maid told her, and with a puzzled frown Prudence set aside her sewing and followed the maid downstairs.

Sir Dudley called to her to enter when she tapped on the door of the room he regarded as his own sanctum, but instead of finding him seated in one of the deep leather armchairs beside the fireplace, her uncle was standing in the middle of the room.

'Come in, my dear,' he said with a smile, and then, with a muttered excuse she did not catch, walked past her and out of the door.

'Uncle — ' she began, and stopped in surprise.

'He is being tactful, my dear,' a deep amused voice came from behind her and she spun round, startled. She had not seen Lord Mottesford, standing in shadow beside the heavily-curtained windows.

'What are you doing here? What do you mean?' she demanded, her heart beginning to beat rapidly.

'Come and sit down,' he replied, and when she did not move walked across to her.

She was too bewildered to resist as he took her hand in his and drew her across to sit in one of the armchairs. He retained her hand and smiled down at her, and her unpredictable heart seemed about to perform acrobatic feats, leaving her breathless and in some indefinable way, afraid.

'Prudence, my dear, I have your uncle's permission, indeed his blessing, for what I have to say. I do not think it will come as any surprise to you, after my loss of control some nights ago at Vauxhall. I know that I offended you greatly then, but I can only plead that I love you so much I was lost to all sense of propriety. Prudence, I love you very dearly, and hope that you can return my regard. Will you agree to become my wife?'

She stared at him, utterly astonished. This was not at all what she had expected. Her heart pounded in her breast and threatened to choke her. For a moment she glimpsed paradise, and knew that this was what above all else she wanted. Then she recalled the reality and was consumed with a bitter, deep anger which hurt more than anything else she had ever experienced.

'How dare you!' she gasped in the end. 'How dare you make such game with me?'

'Game?' he asked, his brows drawn together in a single straight line. 'I don't understand.'

'You can pretend,' Prudence raged at him, her breath now fully restored, 'pretend to love me, when all the while you are concerned with a stupid wager!'

'Wager? What is this, my love,' he demanded, dropping to both knees and attempting to seize her hands in his.

With a frantic sob Prudence evaded him and struggled to her feet, backing away from him across the room.

'Keep away from me!' she exclaimed as he rose and took a step after her. 'Yes, my lord, your wager with Mr Gregory! Oh, don't pretend that you had forgotten it. This is a trick to win, is it not? The month is up today, and having failed to twist me round your little finger, or whatever it was you said you would do, you hope to win by this despicable trick! A hundred pounds! A paltry, miserable hundred pounds! How did you plan to escape once the bet was paid, my lord? Or does winning a disgraceful wager such as you made mean more to you than love? Would you have found some excuse to repudiate the betrothal, or would you have gone through with it, allowing me to believe your lies?'

As he tried to catch her hands in his she twisted away, and with her eyes filled with tears ran towards the door. Oblivious of the astounded Tanner who was walking through the hall, and her aunt who stood at the door of the drawing-room on the first floor, she sped upstairs to her own room, taking a moment to lock the door behind her before she threw herself on to the bed and gave way to tearing, racking sobs.

7

For two days Prudence kept to her room. In truth she was suffering from an incapacitating headache, but it had been brought on by the storm of weeping she had indulged in after Lord Mottesford's proposal.

She had, with some reluctance, opened the door to her aunt, and then had poured out into that astonished lady's ears the account of the wager Netta had overheard.

'He said that he would bring me to heel!' she said furiously. 'Just because I prevented him from beating poor little Harry!'

'When was this?' Lady Frome asked in surprise, and too late Prudence recalled that she and Netta had carefully concealed from her aunt the episode of the broken window.

'It was a month ago,' she explained

slowly. 'We did not want to worry you. The boys were playing cricket in the square, and the ball broke Mr Kennedy's window. He was quite amused, the following day,' she added hurriedly. 'He said that it was a capital shot. But then Harry ran across in front of that man's horses and he caught him and tried to whip him. He's a despicable brute!'

Lady Frome disentangled this speech, and sighed.

'The boys feel so cooped up in town, but Harry must be taught to treat horses with proper care, or he could be hurt.'

'Of course he was to blame, but he's still a baby! There was no need to be so — so vicious about it. And no need at all to treat me as though I were a — a thing for men to make sport of! I'll not be used so!'

'But my dear,' Lady Frome protested, astonished at her vehemence, 'no man would go so far as to offer marriage simply to win such a stupid wager!'

'He would!' Prudence said through gritted teeth. 'He cannot bear to be wrong, or to lose anything!'

'He has asked to see you again,' Lady Frome said mildly, but Prudence shook her head angrily.

'No! What purpose would it serve? This was his last chance, the last day, and it was plain that I was not besotted with him as he had hoped.'

'But if it is as you say, and after today he would lose the wager, what point would there be in pressing the offer?' her aunt asked. 'He must be sincere.'

'He has to pretend that he was. I hate him!' was all that Prudence, at that moment incapable of reasoning logically, would say.

Lady Frome left her alone, knowing that in this intractable mood, which occasionally attacked her normally sensible and equable niece, explanations must wait until Prudence had recovered her composure.

The next day, pale, heavy-eyed, and listless, Prudence came downstairs, although she refused to drive out with her aunt or to discuss Lord Mottesford's offer, saying that it was all at an end and she had no wish ever to hear his name or his offer mentioned again.

When Charlotte came to see how she was, however, exclaiming at her wan looks, she did her utmost to hide her lack of spirits from her friend, saying that she had suffered from a cold.

'But you will be well enough to come to our masquerade, won't you? Charlotte asked urgently. 'I wouldn't dare to wear the toga if you were not there, to give me support by wearing your own.'

'Of course I will come,' Prudence said, although with a heavy heart. Lord Mottesford was bound to be there, and she dreaded meeting him again. If he spoke to her she could not snub him as she would like to do, for that would cause comment and odious speculation. But she determined that neither would she dance with him, nor permit him to speak privately with her.

'Not that he is likely to wish to,' she said under her breath.

'I beg your pardon?' Charlotte asked.

'I'm sorry, I was not attending. Your toga, you asked? I have finished mine.'

'Good. So have I. Emma is practising all day in her hoops,' she confided with a giggle. 'She prances about in her room in front of a mirror, and rehearses going sideways through the dining-room door, because it isn't wide enough for her to pass otherwise.'

'Is your mama going to wear a gown like that?' Prudence asked suddenly, unable to visualise the sight the plump and short Lady Mottesford would present if she donned the wide skirts of her youth.

'No, she has ordered a costume as a shepherdess,' Charlotte revealed. 'It is so short that her ankles show! And she intends to carry a crook, but the problem is that the only one she could find is over six feet high, and it is rather difficult to manage, especially going through doorways.'

Confronted with the image of Lady Mottesford practising carrying her crook through doors where Emma was edging through sideways, Prudence suddenly dissolved into helpless giggles. She must attend the masquerade if only to see this. And she had promised Charlotte, so there was no going back.

She would have to meet Lord Mottesford again some day, unless she wished to spend all her life hidden behind doors, she told herself firmly. It was, after all, his fault in the first place that they were at odds, so if anyone were to be ashamed of the affair it ought to be he.

When the day of the masquerade arrived, however, not even the spectacle afforded by Lady Mottesford, arrayed in sprigged muslin, and coyly displaying her thickening ankles, while clinging as if for support to her crook, and Emma in full sail across the ballroom in a striped pink and yellow damask gown as wide as it was long, could distract Prudence from her nervous anticipation of how Lord Mottesford would behave.

'I do like your toga,' a rather pale Charlotte said, looking at the straight white garment edged with gold braid which Prudence wore so splendidly. 'Mama was furious when she saw mine,' she confided to Prudence as soon as she could detach her friend from the rest of the Frome party. 'She almost sent me back to my room, forbidding me to attend the masquerade, until it occurred to her that it would look decidedly odd if I were not at my own ball.'

'Was she horrid?' Prudence asked sympathetically. 'Did you tell her it was my fault, as I suggested.'

'Of course not. I do not intend to blame you for my actions. I just hate it when she shouts,' Charlotte said with a shudder. 'She used to shout at Papa after they were married. I think it started when Emily — Emma came to live at Trelawn Manor, for I know Papa was angry that he had not been told anything about her. But at least I am not wearing that ghastly dress. I don't care what she does to me afterwards!'

'What can she do?' Prudence said bracingly. 'She will no doubt have forgotten all about it by tomorrow.'

'She threatened to send me away to stay with her brother-in-law, Mr Clutterbuck, so that I would miss the rest of the season,' Charlotte said, swallowing a sob. 'He is a tailor and has a business in Harrow.'

'She cannot do that.'

'She would if she were in a pelter. She doesn't need me so much now that she knows more of the ton. It was only because of my father and his old friends that people were kind to me, and so also had to be friendly to her and Emma, you see,' Charlotte explained simply.

'I don't suppose she will send you away, it would look so foolish if the real reason were to become known, and you can be sure that I would make certain it was,' Prudence declared, a martial light in her eye.

Charlotte sighed. 'I do wish I were as brave as you are,' she said wistfully.

Prudence felt anything but valorous at that precise moment, for she had just seen Lord Mottesford enter the room. Despite his domino and mask, his only concession to costume, he was unmistakable, tall, slim, and with an arrogant air of breeding and command which no disguise could hide.

Swiftly she turned her back, hoping to avoid him for yet a while until she had composed her nerves. It was utterly ridiculous, she chided herself. What, after all, could he do? If he were angry with her he would doubtless not approach her, since there could be little point in quarrelling. Then she could be comfortable.

When the musicians struck up for the first dance she was thankful that her partner was eager to talk, so that she could abandon her unprofitable thoughts. She smiled and flirted, determined to give Lord Mottesford no inkling of how she felt, and was unreasonably piqued when, instead of laying siege to her, he appeared to be enjoying himself enormously, even when dancing with Emma, made ungainly and more than usually maladroit by her lamentable costume.

She was laughingly refusing to reveal her identity to a rather young gallant when, causing her to jump nervously, Lord Mottesford took her arm in a hard, unyielding hand, and spoke softly to her.

'There you are! My dance, I believe. Pray excuse us,' he added to the young man, who blushed and backed hurriedly away as if caught in some social misdemeanour.

'I am not dancing with you!' Prudence hissed angrily, struggling to drag her arm away from his grasp.

'Good, it suits me very well to sit this dance out. Come,' he said calmly, and before she could protest Prudence found herself whisked across the room and through the doors leading to the conservatory.

This was attached to one side of the ballroom, a long, narrow room dimly-illuminated with a few hanging lamps which were virtually lost amidst the profuse foliage, where Lady Mottesford had caused chairs to be placed suggestively in discreetly secluded pairs.

Lord Mottesford led her inexorably past numerous potted palms to the far corner, where they were totally hidden by a bank of exotic flowers and broad-leaved shrubs.

'Sir! Let me go at once!' Prudence demanded, struggling to shake off his hand, but instead of obeying her, Lord Mottesford seized her other hand and drew her towards him.

'You will listen to me!' he said abruptly. 'When I last saw you I was too astounded by what you said to detain you, and you had vanished before I had recovered my wits. How did you know about that ridiculous wager?'

'It is ridiculous, is it, my lord? Can you expect anyone to be pleased at being made the object of such? Especially if the desire to win leads you to such lengths. I could scarce believe Netta when she told me, but she's a truthful child, and you have not denied it.'

'Netta? Your young cousin was there that day? I had not realised. So that explains it, she overheard Edward Gregory making the wager with me, and that is your reason for rejecting my offer. Would it interest you to know that I called off the wager within a week? Soon after I had met you, in fact? When I realised that instead of my first intention of a brief flirtation I knew that you had captivated me, and I wanted you above all else?'

'I don't believe you!' Prudence retorted angrily, unwilling to admit the hope that he loved her, despite his words. 'Gentlemen do not call off wagers, however stupid and humiliating they are!'

'You really think that I would offer marriage in order to win it?' he asked incredulously. 'Or did you imagine that I would collect my winnings and then find some way of escaping from our engagement? Do you think so badly of me?'

'You need say no more,' Prudence replied, still unwilling to be convinced. 'I neither know nor care what you intended, and there is no need to discuss it any further. Now pray release me and permit me to return to the ballroom.'

'Don't be such a little idiot!' he retorted, exasperated. 'I thought no more about the wretched wager and my offer, instead of being a desperate bid to win a paltry hundred pounds, was genuine!'

'Your protestations will do nothing to convince me, my lord!' Prudence said angrily, struggling to free her hands from the firm clasp he had on them.

'Then perhaps this might!' he snapped, and before she could evade him, she found his arms clasped tightly about her, and his lips clamped hard to hers.

Unable to breathe, Prudence felt that she was about to swoon, for she lost all sense of balance and did not know whether she was standing on firm ground or floating in a misty void. His lips were warm, masterful and searching, enticing her own into weak submission, and then the beginnings of a trembling response, as her limbs, after the first outraged stiffening, lost all power of movement as she was moulded to his muscular frame.

He heard the approaching footsteps first and Prudence, shattered by her unexpected reaction to his embrace, found herself suddenly released and thrust into a chair partly concealed by the flourishing greenery. Before she could recover her breath sufficiently to tell him just what she thought of his outrageous behaviour Lady Mottesford's voice penetrated her awareness.

'Dicky? Are you there? Oh, there you

are, my dear boy. I thought I saw you coming this way. You have promised the next dance to dear Emma here, have you not?'

'My dear Aunt,' he said suavely, stepping forward so that they did not come far enough to see Prudence. 'I was admiring the plants. Are they the work of the Frintons, or did you bring them in for the evening?'

'A jungle, is it not?' Lady Mottesford trilled. 'Well, dear boy, it is far more enjoyable to admire the plants in company, so I will leave you with Emma.'

'Let us sit this dance out, Dicky, my dress is so heavy?' Prudence heard Emma say, and before Lord Mottesford could answer she subsided in a frantic rustling of heavy damask draperies on to a seat just behind the plants hiding Prudence. 'Are you enjoying the party?'

'It is unusual,' he replied drily. 'But Cousin Emma, you look hot. I think we would be sensible to go in search of lemonade.'

Emma giggled. 'Oh, Dicky, you are a naughty man. Are you afraid of what people might say if they found us together here? Do you like my costume?'

'It is original,' he replied smoothly, and despite her anger Prudence was almost betrayed into a giggle at the tone of his voice.

'Yes, isn't it?' Emma said complacently, oblivious of his irony. 'There are no more like it. Charlotte was going to wear one just the same, but she would not. The sly little thing made herself a silly Roman toga. Mama was very angry with her, and almost forbade her to attend the masquerade. I think after all I'm glad that she refused to wear it, for it makes me more unusual, doesn't it?'

'Very. But I really do think we need that lemonade. Or would you prefer champagne?'

'Oh, very well, if you insist,' Emma agreed rather petulantly, 'although it will have to be lemonade, for Mama said that the waiters were not to open all the champagne bottles if they could persuade people to drink the fruit cup.'

'Let us go and see what there is,' Lord Mottesford replied, and Prudence heard Emma, her draperies rustling, struggle out of her chair.

'Oh, confound these hoops, they do so get in the way!' Emma exclaimed in annoyance, and Prudence, having by now recovered some equanimity after that shattering embrace, had to stifle a rather hysterical giggle as she cautiously parted the leaves of her screen and peeped through to see Emma bent almost double, her skirts dipping at the front and waving rather frantically at the back, a foot or so off the ground, as she tried to release the hoops which had caught under the arm of another chair.

With Lord Mottesford's bored assistance she freed the gown, but as she straightened, looking up at him and laughing in what, Prudence thought sourly, she no doubt considered a roguish fashion, the heavy skirts of her gown caught the leaves of a plant which was perched on a ledge behind her. Lord Mottesford stretched out an arm to save it, but hampered by Emma's bulky form from reaching it in time, the pot crashed to the floor just as Emma gave a loud moan, put her hand to her head, and swayed sideways.

Lord Mottesford found himself clasping Emma, who had fallen against him and draped her arms about his neck. As he was attempting to disengage himself and lower her to a chair, Prudence heard voices approaching, and looked past them to see Lady Mottesford, accompanied by Sir Tarquin Maltravers, the busiest gossip in London, standing a few feet away.

'Emma? Oh, my dear child!' Lady Mottesford gushed. 'Dicky, how delighted I am! It has been the dearest wish of my heart that you and Emma should fall in love. Come and kiss

Mama, child. You too, Dicky! Oh, this is the happiest day of my life! Come, let us announce it at once. Sir Tarquin, go at once and call for silence. My children, come!'

8

Prudence slipped warily out of the conservatory in the wake of the others. Sir Tarquin had hurried out, gleeful at the thought of being able to announce such astonishing news, and Lady Mottesford, perhaps anxious that his lordship should not have time to reflect, seized one of his arms while Emma hung possessively on to the other. Together they guided him into the ballroom and Prudence, peering anxiously after them, saw that they were approaching the dais at one end on which the musicians sat.

Thankfully she retreated to the other end of the room and mingled with the puzzled guests, scattered from their sets when the music had stopped, rather raggedly, and waiting for whatever was to happen.

'My dear friends,' Lady Mottesford

began, waving her shepherdess's crook above her head as though, Prudence thought, stifling her desire to giggle, she was waving a flag. 'My very dear friends, I know that you will be as pleased as I am to hear my news. My daughter Emma — where are you, Emi — Emma, my love? — is going to follow in my footsteps. No, I don't mean that, exactly, but she is going to be the second Lady Emma Mottesford. She is going to marry my dear, lamented husband's heir, Dicky. Come here, Dicky, hold Emma's hand now. Here, ladies and gentlemen, are the happy couple.'

Prudence felt nauseated. Would Lord Mottesford repudiate this engagement? As she had suspected him of being prepared to do if she had accepted him? He had been trapped, it was clear, but he could still explain that it had been a misunderstanding. He did not seem about to speak, however, and there was little time for conjecture as a buzz of conversation rose from the guests.

'Ye Gods!' a man beside Prudence ejaculated. 'No-one ever calls him Dicky! Ugh! The fellow must be foxed to even think of offering for such an antidote!'

'Hush, George,' his wife whispered urgently, but Prudence overheard similar remarks from others nearby, and it was the sole topic of conversation for the remainder of the evening, apart from disgusted comments that even to celebrate such an amazing success for her daughter Lady Mottesford had provided no more champagne.

'It's monstrous!' Sarah complained when she encountered Prudence an hour later. 'It's unbelievable that a man like Mottesford should even think of marrying so vulgar a creature as Emma Potter. That woman is already preening herself unbearably, talking of the future Lady Emma, if you please. You'd think she would have learned by now that she won't be Lady Emma, only Lady Mottesford.'

'I wonder if she had realised it will

make her the dowager?' Mrs Buxton asked with a chuckle. 'Oh, dear, it's dreadful! What could Richard have been thinking of?'

'It serves him right!' Prudence said coldly, but refused to elaborate on this statement, even to herself, until she was alone.

The remainder of the masquerade had passed with infinite slowness for Prudence, who felt that the fixed smile on her face must either be clamped there for ever, or break her head in two.

It had ended at last, however, but the news had spread to the Fromes' house before the Fromes themselves returned there, and Prudence had been forced to endure the exclamations and speculations of her maid as the girl prepared her for bed.

At last she was alone. Her chief feeling was of numbness. It was followed by a mixture of despair as she finally confessed to herself that despite all her doubts of him she had grown to love Lord Mottesford, and bitter triumph that, after his plot to ensnare her, he had himself been so neatly trapped by the even more unscrupulous Lady Mottesford. Suddenly she began to laugh, at first silently, then with gathering hysteria which she fought to control as she buried her face in the pillows. At last the shuddering which had convulsed her body subsided and she lay quietly, totally drained of all emotion.

Forcing herself to appear as normal the following day, she had to endure Netta's demanding curiosity, and relate what had happened to her young cousin. She omitted the scene in the conservatory, for to reveal it would lead to questions as to what she herself had been doing there, and that was impossible to answer.

However trying she thought Netta's interest, she found it even more irksome to withstand the glances of sympathy from her aunt, and maintain her pretence that she had never cared for

Lord Mottesford.

It was therefore with some relief that she welcomed Charlotte late that afternoon. It seemed that no-one could talk of anything else, for all their morning callers had been full of the news. Indeed Prudence suspected that many of them, having seen Lord Mottesford in her company rather frequently, came with the malicious intention of watching to see how she was reacting to the loss of one of her most constant suitors. At least from Charlotte she would hear whether her mama and Emma were as satisfied as they had appeared the previous evening.

Charlotte, however, was pale and looked distraught. Prudence was alone in the morning room, attempting to read and distract herself from her thoughts, when Tanner showed her in.

'Charlotte, whatever is the matter?' Prudence demanded when she saw her friend.

'It's — it's Mama!' Charlotte exclaimed, and promptly burst into tears.

It was some considerable time before she was calm enough to talk, and her explanation was punctuated with isolated sobs and hiccups.

'Mr Gregory called this morning,' she said after a while. 'Oh, Prudence, he offered for me!'

'Well, if you like him, and I think you do, that is no need for tears!' Prudence said bracingly, firmly suppressing thoughts of the offer she had herself received.

'Oh, I do, I do, and above all things I would like to marry him, but that is the point. Mama says that I cannot!'

'Cannot? What does she mean? Surely if he has offered he must know that you are not rich, and be willing to accept that?'

'Yes, he says that he does not care about my lack of fortune,' Charlotte said with a gulp. 'I know that it was wrong, but we could not help ourselves, truly we could not, and he spoke to me, told me last night, that he wished to offer for me, and would see Mama today.'

'Well? What happened?'

'He came, and there was the most dreadful row. It was Mama, she shouted and called him the vilest names, saying that he had no right to speak to me first. I was in the back drawing-room, and heard it all, for they did not know I was there. I had gone to get a book, you see, and he was shown in before I could leave, and to go would have made a noise since the door squeaks. Besides, when I heard what she said I could not have gone. Oh, Prudence, what shall I do?'

'Calmly, tell me what she said about not accepting this offer,' Prudence urged, her own troubles forgotten in the need to console Charlotte.

Charlotte took a deep breath, and went on more steadily.

'He said he wished to offer for me, and thought that I would be willing. That was when she began to abuse him for not obtaining her permission to speak to me. He ignored that, and went on to say that his fortune was not large, but his estates were unencumbered, and he could provide me with a comfortable home.'

'Well, what reason did she give for refusing him?' Prudence asked. 'Surely the mere fact that he had already approached you could not weigh so heavily with her?'

'She said — Oh, Prudence, I can't bear it!' Charlotte gasped, and once more dissolved into a flood of tears.

'Tell me,' Prudence said gently, and gradually Charlotte resumed her story.

'She said that I was already promised!'

'What? How can that be?' Prudence exclaimed.

'Hubert!' Charlotte wailed, and this time her bout of tears was so unrestrained that for a time Prudence thought that she would have to send for help. Eventually, however, Charlotte became calm, and begged pardon for being such a watering pot.

'You would never agree to marry him!' Prudence declared fervently.

Charlotte sighed, her tears no longer flowing.

'I dislike him so much. Indeed he makes me shiver with revulsion every time he touches me. And he is always making excuses to touch my hands, or take my arm, helping me, with that horrid smile on his face!'

'Then you must refuse to marry him. They cannot force you to do so,' Prudence urged.

'She can, for I am not strong like you. She says that if I am obstinate she will take me to Devon, to the dower house which Papa left her, and lock me away with only bread and water until I submit. Prudence, truly I would kill myself rather than marry Hubert!'

'That would not be of much use,' Prudence rallied her. 'Come, if she threatens this we must make plans. Would Edward elope with you?'

'Oh, I couldn't!' she exclaimed,

shocked. 'And he would not dream of asking me to,' she added.

Prudence frowned. After his part in the wager she had little doubt that Edward Gregory would be prepared to defy convention, but Charlotte could not. She was not the stuff of which heroines were made. Some other way would have to be found.

'Have you any other relatives? Anyone at all that you could go to, who would either take your part or hide you?' she asked, but Charlotte shook her head dolefully.

'The only other relative I have is Lord Mottesford, and now that he is to marry Emma he will not be prepared to defy Mama. Besides, he does not like me.'

'I did not know that Emma wanted him,' Prudence said, momentarily diverted from Charlotte's problems.

'Oh, yes, she always has. Mama was angry that he inherited the title, and Trelawn Manor. She does not understand about entails. Mama once said that it would be fitting if he married one of us, but although I had a better right to Papa's money than Emma, it was unwise for cousins to marry. Then she said that if she considered me her daughter there was no reason why Papa should not have considered Emma to be his, therefore he should have left us equally provided for. She was determined to recover what Cousin Richard had inherited, and besides, he was rich before Papa died.'

'Have you any friends?' Prudence asked, dragging her mind back from this ingenuous revelation of Lady Mottesford's mercenary designs.

'Only Miss Jackson. She used to be my governess, when I was small, and she writes to me quite often. She stayed longer than any of the later ones, for she was not afraid of Papa.'

'She sounds the right sort of person, but how can a governess help you? She will be living in someone else's home,' Prudence pointed out.

'Not Miss Jackson. You see, she

inherited a legacy, and she and her sister were able to set up a small school in Bath. That is why she left me.'

'Could you go to her?'

'Yes, I am sure she would hide me, but how could I go? I have no money, and I would be afraid to travel alone on the stage.'

Prudence's eyes were gleaming.

'I'll dress as your maid and come with you. As for money, I have just had my quarter's allowance and I have plenty. But what about Mr Gregory? I know, you must write to him and he can either persuade your mama that she must permit the marriage to prevent a scandal, or come to Bath and marry you there.'

'I dare not!' Charlotte said, but Prudence had little difficulty in persuading her that it was the only thing to do. Charlotte was so terrified of being forced into wedlock with Hubert that she was desperate enough to take steps which her normally timid nature would have shrunk from.

'We'll take the stage tomorrow morning,' Prudence said, busy already with plans. 'Sit down now and write to Edward, and I will arrange that he receives it tomorrow morning.'

'No, I cannot go so soon!' Charlotte protested. 'Ought I not to write to Miss Jackson first to see whether she is willing to receive me?'

'She might write to your mama,' Prudence warned. 'But in any case her letter to you might be intercepted by Lady Mottesford. If you simply appear on her doorstep there is little she can do except take you in, and after you have seen her she is bound to be prepared to help.'

'And I think it would be better if I saw Edward to explain, too,' Charlotte said slowly. 'He usually rides in the park every morning, and I can slip out of the house, or tell Mama that I am walking with you. She and Emma are so busy planning bride clothes that they will not pay much heed to what I am doing.'

'Yes, and perhaps you should not

oppose the suggestion of Hubert, to throw them off the scent. I don't mean agree to it,' she added hurriedly as Charlotte turned startled eyes towards her, 'just seem uncaring, as though you are becoming resigned and cannot be too much against it.'

Although Prudence was sorry for the delay, she knew that it was partly her own desire to escape for a short while from the curious looks of her acquaintances that made her anxious to leave London. There seemed no great urgency, for with the announcement of Emma's wedding Lady Mottesford would be unlikely to wish to leave London too soon, and she was so confident of her own cleverness that she would be totally unsuspicious of Charlotte's uncharacteristic rebellion.

Their plans suffered the first setback when, having walked in the park for long hours on three consecutive days without a glimpse of Edward, Prudence learned through Sarah that he had left London.

'Where has he gone? When does he mean to return?' she demanded, and was not greatly comforted when told that he would be away for another two days only.

Charlotte was terrified that he would not come back, and to distract her Prudence persuaded her to write a letter to Edward which could be sent to his rooms to await his homecoming.

'Mama says she will send a notice of betrothals to 'The Gazette' next week,' she told Prudence on the following day.

'That will be too late, she cannot do it if you have disappeared. I wondered why Emma's betrothal had not yet been announced,' she said with as casual an air as she could manage.

'She — Mama, and Cousin Richard have been trying to arrange where the wedding is to be,' Charlotte explained. 'Cousin Richard wants to announce the date and place when the betrothal is notified, but he wants to marry in Worcestershire and Emma insists on being married at St George's, Hanover Square. Mama is trying to find somewhere they can both agree on, and she now wants it to be at Trelawn Manor. She said Hubert and I could marry there, too, at the same time.'

Suppressing her own anguish, Prudence wondered briefly who would win this battle of wills, then she turned her attention to plans for the journey to Bath, packing a small valise with necessities for both of them, since Charlotte would be less able to smuggle what she needed out of the house, and writing a letter to be left for her aunt, explaining what she was doing and the necessity for it.

'She will understand,' she reassured Charlotte. 'She is never angry with me for long, it is too fatiguing for her, and she has said what a ghastly man Hubert is.'

'I wish Edward were back,' Charlotte sighed.

'The day after tomorrow. Shall we walk in the park in the morning?'

'The last time?' Charlotte asked wistfully.

'Yes, until you are Edward's wife, and then you can come to town every year if you wish.'

'I must do some shopping first, and then I will come straight to the park. Shall we meet in the usual place?'

'Very well. I will be there. Are you going to the theatre this evening?'

Lady Mottesford, with Emma and Charlotte, and also Hubert, was there, preening herself and waving to every slight acquaintance, but Lord Mottesford was not escorting them. Prudence noted this with some puzzlement. She had not seen him since the masquerade, and wondered whether he had gone out of town with Edward Gregory, or was hiding from his friends in embarrassment at the trap he had fallen into.

On the following morning Prudence and Sarah went early to the park, but Charlotte did not appear at the agreed time. Prudence paced slowly up and down, chatting to acquaintances, but all the time looking about her for her friend.

'Prudence, pay heed!' Sarah exclaimed in annoyance. 'Here is Lord Mottesford, with a new pair of chestnuts, by the looks of it. I haven't seen him for an age, not since that frightful masquerade party. What on earth could have induced him to offer for the dreadful Emma? Not at all the sort of thing he was expected to do.'

Prudence looked round, to find him drawing up alongside them. He greeted them brusquely.

'Miss Lee, pray drive with me for a few minutes,' he said abruptly, and Prudence was so taken aback that she was unable to think of a way of refusing before she had, with Sarah's swift encouragement, been helped up into the curricle.

He drove off slowly, without speaking, a frown on his face. Then, as if making a decision, he turned towards her, his face stern. Before he could speak however, Prudence heard her name being called and looked round to see Netta running wildly towards them, Biddy in breathless pursuit.

'What is it?' she demanded, as Netta, panting, halted beside the curricle.

'Charlotte! She gave James this note to give to either me or you. They were leaving, all of them, and Hubert, and there was another coach piled high with baggage,' Netta gasped, thrusting a screw of paper into Prudence's hand.

Prudence paled, and hastily straightened the note.

'Lady Mottesford found a copy of Charlotte's letter to Edward, and is taking her down to Devon,' she said blankly. 'She will force her to marry Hubert as soon as they reach Trelawn Manor. No! She must not! I must stop her!'

9

'If you please!'

Lord Mottesford calmly took the note from Prudence and swiftly scanned it. She scarcely noticed, her thougts intent on devising a means to avert this calamity.

'What is so important about this note to Edward?' he asked curtly.

Prudence stared at him, for the moment uncomprehending, but Netta answered.

'He offered for her, and her mama refused him, saying that she was already promised to the hateful Hubert! And it wasn't true, at least Charlotte had not agreed to it. Why, she did not even know that he had offered, just that her mama wanted them to marry. Poor Charlotte, how will she bear it?'

'She won't. I must help her, but how can I get to her?' Prudence fretted. 'Oh, if only we had run away when we first thought of the scheme!'

'Run away?' Netta demanded, her eyes widening. 'Oh, Pru, you were planning to run away with Charlotte and you never told me!'

Lord Mottesford ignored this.

'When did they leave? How long ago?' he asked sharply, and Netta turned back to him eagerly.

'Will you chase them?' she demanded. 'Oh, can I come with you? Will you challenge Hubert to a duel?'

'Yes, no and no,' he replied impatiently. 'For pity's sake, child, answer me if you want to help Charlotte!'

Netta gulped. 'It was about an hour ago,' she said in a small, subdued voice. 'I came to find Pru as soon as I knew about it. You see, James and Harry were playing cricket, and they did not come in at once. And I had been in the schoolroom with Miss Francis so I did not actually see them leave. Do you think you can catch them?'

'They will travel slowly, I should be able to come up with them by the second stage, and bring Charlotte back to town tonight.'

Netta grinned. 'Well, even if you don't have a duel with Hubert I hope you draw his cork,' she said with bloodthirsty anticipation.

'Thank you. I will do my utmost to satisfy your ideas of vengeance! Now will you please do something for me, Prudence? Edward is due back this morning. Can you see him and explain, and ask him to follow me. The Staines and Bagshot road, though I ought to have come up with them long before then.'

'No. I'm coming with you.'

'Of course you cannot! Don't be ridiculous!' Lord Mottesford exclaimed, but Prudence turned to him, a pleading look in her eye.

'Pray consider! Charlotte will be alone, so terrified! She will need someone she trusts. And if you maintain that we can be back in town by this evening, what harm can there be?'

He gave her a long, searching look, then nodded.

'Netta, can you take your maid and visit Mr Gregory, show him Charlotte's note, and tell him what we're doing?' he asked briskly and Netta, thrilled with taking part in such exciting events, nodded eagerly. Lord Mottesford told her the address, made sure that both she and Biddy knew how to find it, and with a cheerful wave turned his curricle and set off in the direction of Kensington.

Relieved to have crossed this first hurdle, Prudence remained silent as, without appearing to hasten, Lord Mottesford threaded his way through the fashionable strollers, nodding occasionally to friends, but resisting all invitations to halt, until they left the park. Then he urged his chestnuts, a magnificently powerful pair, into a gallop until they reached the small village and had to slow down to negotiate the narrow main street.

Once past the houses he let the chestnuts have their heads. They were fresh and eager, and soon the curricle was bowling along, delayed only when they had to pause before overtaking the slower carts and coaches. Prudence sat quietly, admiring his skill with the ribbons, and merely holding on to the curricle for support when he feather-edged a corner or cut in between a huge lumbering coach and a wagon coming the other way, with only inches to spare.

When they reached more open road he glanced across at her, a smile of amusement on his face.

'You appear to have been in Charlotte's confidence. When did Edward make his offer?'

'A few days ago, the morning after the masquerade,' Prudence replied, blushing as she recalled the various embarrassing happenings there. 'Lady Mottesford told him that Charlotte was already promised to Hubert. I still cannot understand it,' she added in a puzzled manner.

'And this plan to run away?'

'She has a friend, a former governess, who would have helped her. She was planning to go to her and I said I would accompany her on the stage, pretending to be her maid, because I could not have let her travel on her own. But she wanted to tell Edward herself and, as he has been out of town, we could not contrive to meet him.'

'Could Lady Mottesford have had wind of this plot?' he asked, his tone amused.

'It is unlikely, for we told no-one else. But why should she suddenly take it into her head to travel all the way to Devon?'

'Her objectives so far as Emma was concerned had been achieved, and to remain in town would have been expensive. My aunt does not enjoy spending money, except on herself,' he added drily, and Prudence cast a swift look at his face. He was staring straight

157

ahead and she could detect nothing in his expression. He went on, 'As for Charlotte, her presence was necessary to obtain entry into the ton, but I imagine that all along she intended her nephew to marry the chit.'

'But why?' Prudence exclaimed. 'Charlotte has so small a fortune, that could not have been Hubert's motive. And as I understand it they had not met before she came to town, so he could not have fallen in love with her before. Not that such a creature could ever love anyone but himself!' she added caustically.

'Did Charlotte tell you her fortune was small?' he asked. 'Does she know exactly what it is?'

'She had no idea, but her mama told her it was not enough to attract anyone. And that there was only enough income from it to buy a few dresses, which is why Charlotte was always so shabbily dressed and had almost no pin money! Lady Mottesford would hardly be willing to spend any of her own money on the poor child, and even though she complains that you inherited almost everything as well as what was entailed, she must have had a considerable sum from what Charlotte has said!'

He was silent for a moment while he negotiated a tricky bend and overtook a chaise. Then he glanced at Prudence.

'My late uncle's widow has been busy,' he commented. 'I understand that Lady Mottesford has control over Charlotte's money until she is married, or reaches the age of thirty. She cannot touch the principle, which is vested in Charlotte from her own mother, but she must be removing a considerable proportion of the interest each year, as well as the three of them living on it.'

'You mean that Charlotte is wealthy and does not know it?' Prudence gasped.

'She inherited forty thousand from her mother,' he replied evenly. 'Plus the accumulated interest, for her father was a miser with her money as well as his own, and while he had control over it spent as little as possible.'

Prudence was gasping. 'Why, she is an heiress! So that is why the wretched woman is so determined to marry her to Hubert, to keep the money in her own family. Probably she would not even then allow Charlotte to know what her fortune was, and with Hubert's connivance they would be able to use it themselves! Oh, how wicked!'

'Apart from her mother's money, which he had no power over for his own disposal, and the single estate of Trelawn Manor, which was entailed, her father left everything to Lady Mottesford. And he was worth far more than forty thousand!'

Prudence stared at him in speechless amazement, and for several minutes remained silent, thinking of the enormity of the deceit which her stepmother had practised on Charlotte.

'Oh, they are wicked! How can people be so avaricious, so deceitful? They deserve to be thrown into the vilest prison there is!' she exclaimed after a while.

'Unfortunately, despicable and unfair though we consider it, she is within her rights,' he replied evenly. 'She inherited my uncle's money quite legally, and as well as being named Charlotte's guardian was given sole control over her fortune.'

Prudence had recalled suddenly that he was himself betrothed to Emma, however much he had been trapped into it, and she eyed him speculatively. Was he hoping to acquire some of his late uncle's money through such a marriage, or would he repudiate the engagement, she wondered, and then firmly advised herself not to think about that. He could not wish to marry her. Whatever had been his motive for renewing his proposal on the night of the masquerade her vehement refusal of it must have driven him away.

She sighed, and this time it was Lord Mottesford who glanced curiously at her, although he did not speak.

They lapsed into silence while he concentrated on driving, and Prudence began to devise plans for Charlotte's rescue. He paused briefly at the first major posting house to make inquiries and discovered that the equipage had indeed halted there about 40 minutes earlier. Lady Mottesford, with her usual talent for attracting attention, was recalled by a grinning ostler who informed them how she had loudly demanded that the landlord in person bring her and her companions glasses of ratafia. When that worthy, pre-occupied in dealing with travellers from a mail coach which had arrived seconds before, delegated this task to an underling, Lady Mottesford had declared her intention never again to patronise the inn.

'And good riddance, for ne'er a groat did she gi' us!' he finished, eyeing the guinea Lord Mottesford was finger-ing.

'Did they say where they would change next?' he asked the man, but the ostler shook his head.

'Don't suppose they knew theirselves. But they might stop to bait at the Swan in Staines.'

'My thanks.'

Lord Mottesford tossed him the coin, and swung out of the yard.

'Good, we're catching up with them, they are not travelling particularly swiftly. I expect they are planning to take three days on the journey, and stay the first night at Andover.'

They crossed the river, but Lord Mottesford did not halt to make any further inquiries now that they knew they were on the right road. His chestnuts performed magnificently for two stages, and when he stopped to change them he left strict instructions for their care and promised to send his groom to collect them on the following day.

He also insisted on pausing to take some refreshments, although Prudence, becoming anxious, would have pressed on.

'Ten minutes will make little difference. Come, a slice of pie and a glass of wine will revive you.'

The new pair, bays, were the best that could be had, but they were by no means so fast as the chestnuts. Their speed fell considerably, and when Lord Mottesford halted at Bagshot he learned that Lady Mottesford's chaise had passed through 15 minutes earlier.

Several miles farther on they entered the pretty village of Hartney Witney, and Prudence exclaimed as she saw a post chaise standing outside a small inn facing the village green.

Lord Mottesford drew up the sweating bays and tossed the reins to an ostler, telling him to wait until he had been inside the inn.

Prudence scrambled down after him, certain that they had found their quarry.

As she followed Lord Mottesford into the inn she heard the sound of a loud, querulous voice and the high pitched whine of a woman. She found herself in a dark, stone-flagged passageway with doors to either side. Lord Mottesford was standing just inside the doorway, and Prudence squeezed into the space beside him in order to see what was causing the commotion.

Hubert, his many-caped cloak almost filling the passageway, was haranguing the innkeeper. This was a small wiry man who was standing in an open doorway at the end of the passage, through which Prudence caught glimpses of a huge kitchen. Behind Hubert, wringing her hands in anxiety, was a skinny woman, not much more than a girl, who punctuated Hubert's tirade with frantic assertions that she hadn't done anything.

At that moment, before Hubert was aware of the newcomers, Lady Mottesford appeared in the doorway to the left of the passage.

'What is the delay? Hurry, fellow, I want a luncheon straight away. I'm swooning with lack of food after hours in a chaise!'

'I'm just explainin' to that nodcock,' the innkeeper said angrily, jerking his head in Hubert's direction, 'that it takes time to roast a capon or a turkey. You're welcome to a slice of cold ham, or beef, or an omelette, and I've plenty o'pies, but that's all I can do unless you're willin' to wait!'

'Bring what you can, fellow,' Lady Mottesford said curtly. 'Hubert, there's no use arguing with yokels, they don't cater for the quality in these rustic hovels.'

'Good day to you,' Lord Mottesford interrupted quietly as she turned to step back inside the room, and Lady Mottesford swung round, her mouth open in astonishment.

'My — my lord! What are you doing here?' she gasped, clutching at the neck of her pale blue pelisse as if to give herself more air.

'That is something I need to ask you,' he replied smoothly. 'But in private, I think,' he added, moving forward so purposefully that she gave way before him. Prudence swiftly followed him through into a small coffee room, which looked even smaller as he dominated it.

'Here, what the devil is this?' Hubert demanded, recovering from his astonishment and rushing in after them.

'Prudence!' Charlotte shrieked, as she dropped Fifi, which she had been clutching to her, and rose from the stool where she had been crouching to run across the room and fling herself into her friend's arms, bursting into tears as she did so.

'Dicky!' Emma exclaimed, her initial look of apprehension changing to a coy simper as she rose from the windowseat and tripped across the room towards him.

He turned to look at her, his eyes hard and cold, and she paused, then laughed slightly.

'Do let us all be comfortable,' she urged. 'Dicky, come and sit beside me. It is such a delightful surprise to see you, although I cannot imagine what Miss Lee is doing with you?'

'Can't you, by gad!' Hubert muttered, then stepped back hastily as Lord Mottesford swung round towards him, his hands clenched.

'Keep your thoughts to yourself, puppy! Now, your ladyship, I wish to know why you left town so hurriedly?' he added, turning back to where Lady Mottesford, arms akimbo, stood facing him across the door.

'I don't have to answer to you,' she was beginning heatedly when Emma, casting a placating look towards Lord Mottesford, caught her hand.

'Mama, no doubt Dicky was worried about me,' she said urgently, but her words were unheeded.

'I am Charlotte's guardian,' her mama was saying truculently, 'and no-one has the right to dictate to me what arrangements I make for her.'

'What arrangements have you made, may I ask?' Lord Mottesford asked smoothly.

'I — she's to wed my nephew,' was the reply.

'This — er — tailor's dummy?' Lord Mottesford asked with studied insolence.

'I demand satisfaction for that insult!' Hubert shouted, but his aunt shouted more loudly.

'There's no cause, my lord, for you to sneer, or for anyone to say it's an unequal match. Hubert's papa is in a very nice way of business, I'll have you know, and Hubert will inherit that. And if Charlotte's papa can marry me, there's no call for you or anyone to turn your nose up at Hubert!'

'You may in law be Charlotte's guardian, but as head of the family, I intend to exercise my right to ensure that she is not forced into any match against her will! Do you wish to marry this creature?' he asked, turning to Charlotte, who was sobbing quietly in Prudence's arms.

'Of course not!' she hiccuped, 'I want to marry Edward!'

'Then you shall, so dry your eyes now, and I will take you back to

London until it can be arranged.'

'So that's it!' Hubert, frustrated at being ignored, suddenly exclaimed. 'That fellow Gregory's a pal of yours, isn't he, and no doubt you're planning on getting Charlotte's fortune for him!'

'I haven't any fortune!' Charlotte was beginning, but Lord Mottesford's voice cut across hers.

'I'd sooner he have it than see you fritter it away, as no doubt you would. I've been told of your expensive tastes, in women as well as clothes! A pity you don't look better for all the blunt you drop!'

'Why, you — you — '

Words failed Hubert, and he suddenly leaped forward, his arms flailing, aiming punches wildly at Lord Mottesford's head.

Charlotte, Emma and Lady Mottesford shrieked in unison, Fifi barked deliriously, Prudence stepped back swiftly, out of range, pulling Charlotte with her, and Lord Mottesford, with what seemed to the bemused watchers no more than a slight jab with his left fist at Hubert's jaw, sent him crashing senseless to the floor just as the landlord, carrying an enormous tray, flung open the door and entered the room.

10

Ten minutes later order had been restored. Hubert sat on a settle beside the fireplace nursing his jaw, casting darkling glances at Lord Mottesford, but uttering nothing. Lady Mottesford had finally run out of abusive remarks which for the first few minutes she had hurled nonstop at his lordship, and was seated at the table where the landlord had finally deposited the food. Prudence and Charlotte sat together on the windowseat, as far removed from the others as possible, Fifi fast asleep on Charlotte's lap, and gently snoring, while Emma, also seated at the table, looked admiringly up at her betrothed.

Lord Mottesford, who had stood unmoved while the storm about him had raged, looked sardonically at Hubert then turned slowly towards Charlotte.

'I understand that you do not know what your fortune is,' he said quietly.

'It is not fitting for young girls to be involved in such matters,' Lady Mottesford said hastily. 'Time enough for that when they are old enough to understand, and not waste it.'

'Or never to be told, is that it? Charlotte, your mother's fortune is worth over forty thousand pounds, plus interest which was being reinvested in the funds by your father.'

'Forty thousand?' Charlotte gasped. 'That means that I am rich! The interest — surely it was more than she said?'

'Much more,' he agreed. 'I shall expect your stepmother to account to me for how she has dealt with it since your papa died.'

'Then you'll expect for nothing!' Lady Mottesford retorted. 'I've sole control.'

'To use it for Charlotte's advantage,' he pointed out softly. 'I do not think keeping her in rags while you and your daughter deck yourselves in jewels and expensive finery could be called that. I shall make absolutely certain that, out of your own very ample fortune, you repay what you have appropriated.'

'That's slander!' she spluttered. 'I'll sue you, my fine lord, making such insinuations against a poor widow woman!'

'A rich one, my lady, and my lawyers may have different opinions to yours. Charlotte, do you wish to eat or shall we leave at once? I am taking you back to town.'

'You can't do this!' Lady Mottesford wailed, struggling to her feet. 'I'm her guardian!'

'Dicky, you can't mean to leave me like this!' Emma cried out, trying to catch his hand, but he had moved towards the door.

'Oh, please!' Charlotte whispered, clasping Prudence's hand tightly. 'Please, Cousin Richard, take me away!'

'Very well. Are your boxes here or on the other coach?'

'I have just a small valise, the rest of my things are on the other coach,' Charlotte said. 'What shall we do? It was going to take much longer to get to Devon.'

'Your stepmother will have to send the rest back then. Come, we will go and find the valise.'

Charlotte rose to her feet, went towards the door, and then turned back.

'My jewel box,' she said breathlessly. 'I had it with me, and brought it into here for safety. Where is it?'

She saw it on a small side table and with a sigh of relief stepped forward to take it. At the same time Lady Mottesford reached across and picked up the box.

'No, you'll not have them! It's not fitting that a chit like you should have control of jewels.'

'It's not really a jewel box,' Charlotte cried, trying to take the box away from her. 'I have a few trinkets, but it's the box Papa gave me, the only thing I have of his! Give it to me!'

She tugged suddenly, and Fifi, excited, leaped up and down and bit Lady Mottesford on her ankle. She kicked out and shouted, and between them they dropped the box, which fell with ominous sounds of rending wood on to the hard boards. Prudence, who had been standing behind Charlotte, stepped forwards and bent to retrieve the box while Emma rushed to succour her moaning parent.

'The bottom seems to have come unstuck,' Prudence said.

'It should be possible to repair it, Charlotte. Oh, there's a paper in here. Is it yours?'

'I put no papers there,' Charlotte said, puzzled, taking the box from Prudence. 'Why, look, there's a small compartment underneath the main one, that's where the paper was.'

'Permit me,' Lord Mottesford said, retrieving the paper seconds before Lady Mottesford could reach for it.

'I'll kill that dratted dog! Let me

alone, Emma, I'm not dying! As for you, spying on a girl's love letters, it's disgusting!' Lady Mottesford sniffed, and while Charlotte angrily denied this, Lord Mottesford ignored it.

He spread out the thick sheets and carefully read what was written on them, then looked up slowly at Charlotte.

'Your father gave you this box?' he asked.

'Yes, the day before he died. Why, what is the paper?'

'Did you know of this secret compartment?'

'No, I had no notion it was there.'

'What a pity. Here, this is your father's last letter to you. Read it.'

Charlotte complied, and then raised puzzled eyes to her cousin.

'I don't understand. He says he is sorry for not being a good father to me and that he was constrained to make out a will leaving everything that was not entailed to his wife. He secretly made another will, to leave everything to me apart from a small jointure for her. Is it true?'

Lord Mottesford nodded.

'Here is the will, properly phrased although clearly he did it himself. And properly witnessed, by the housekeeper and butler at Trelawn Manor, if my memory of their names serves correctly.'

'It's false, a trick! I didn't! It's my money! I worked hard for it!' Lady Mottesford raved, trying to snatch the will which Lord Mottesford held contemptuously out of reach.

'So, my fine lady, you are unmasked!' he said coldly. 'This will appoints me his executor and Charlotte's guardian. You are to have the dower house for the rest of your life, and sufficient income to maintain it. I suggest that you go there at once, and I will visit you in a few days when you are calmer to discuss what is to be done as regards repaying Charlotte what you have misused of her money. I doubt whether you will dare to show your face in London again.'

Lady Mottesford, to the embarrassment of Charlotte and Prudence, dissolved into floods of tears. Hubert glared at her, while Emma patted her hand ineffectually.

'Never mind, Mama. It wasn't your doing if that horrid old man broke his promise to you. And people will not blame you, there is no need for you to hide away in Devon. Dicky is rich even without that money, and when we are married you shall come and stay with me in London.'

She glanced up at Lord Mottesford as she spoke, half coyly, half placatingly, but he gave her no answering smile.

'I think not, Miss Potter. After my marriage I mean to retrench. I intend to close all my houses apart from a small farmhouse in Westmorland where you will live. I shall, of course, need to travel about myself to oversee the estates, but I will doubtless find time to visit you almost every year for a few days. It's a very lonely spot, unfortunately, but you will be at home in the village there. No trips to London, however.'

'What?' Emma gasped incredulously. 'You'd banish me on my own to some dreary farmhouse hundreds of miles away? I don't believe you!'

'I never make idle threats. When we are married that is what your life will have to be. But don't be concerned, there are half a dozen other houses in the village, and a couple of women around your age. Of course, they are uneducated, and there are no books, and certainly no parties, but there is a great deal to do on the farm, baking, brewing, milking, cutting hay for the cattle, and looking after the sheep, especially in winter. You'd never be bored.'

'No, for I have no intention of living such a life!' Emma retorted angrily.

'That is how I say you will live,' he replied calmly. 'It may not be to your liking, but I think that if we spend nothing apart from on essentials we may be able to spend a week in Carlisle in a few years. They have quite fashionable assemblies, I am told.'

'You don't understand!' she cried furiously. 'I'll not do it! I'll not marry you! You misled me, I thought you were rich! Not even a title would make up for that sort of life.'

'Well, perhaps it would be best. How fortunate that we made no announcement in 'The Gazette'. Now, Mr Clutterbuck, I asked the landlord to put to your horses, so I suggest you escort the ladies on their way. Charlotte, come with me to show me which is your valise. Goodbye, Lady Mottesford, Miss Potter. I will call in a week or so to arrange about repayment of Charlotte's money.'

He swept out of the room, Charlotte's hand firmly held in his, and Prudence heard him outside talking to the postilion. Within the coffee room Lady Mottesford was looking dazed, Emma seemed on the verge of hysterics, and Mr Clutterbuck was muttering threats about getting even one day with a damned chiselling, cheating gallows-cheat.

By the time Lord Mottesford returned, however, they had pulled themselves together enough to collect their belongings and, as he politely held the door open for them, walk with as much dignity as they could muster out to their carriage.

Charlotte watched them go, and then stood looking through the window until the chaise was out of sight. Then she turned to look with some awe at Lord Mottesford.

'Cousin Richard, I don't know how to thank you! I think I would have died rather than marry Hubert. And I am rich! I can't believe it! Oh, when is Edward coming back to town.'

'I left word for him to follow us,' Lord Mottesford said soothingly. 'In fact, there is someone arriving now. Yes,' he added after a swift look through the window. 'Charlotte, listen to me, quickly. If you heed my advice don't tell Edward that you have a large fortune until after he has offered for you. He's a

182

plaguey touchy fellow, he might think he couldn't marry an heiress. Do you understand?'

Charlotte nodded swiftly, and then turned eagerly to the door as it was flung impetuously open and Edward Gregory marched in.

'Well, what sort of a coil is this?' he demanded, striding across the room to take Charlotte's hand in his. 'Netta was full of bogeymen and wicked witches, I thought you'd all been dragged off to some enchanted forest.'

Laughing and crying, Charlotte tried to explain, until Prudence took pity on her and spoke.

'Lady Mottesford refused your offer because she wanted Charlotte to marry Hubert,' she said crisply. 'They were travelling to Devon in order to force her compliance, and Lord Mottesford and I chased them. He prevented it,' she finished, beginning to laugh at the recollection. 'He knocked Hubert down, and was marvellous!'

'My thanks, Richard,' Edward said,

still looking puzzled. 'Where are they?'

'On their way to Devon,' Lord Mottesford said calmly.

'But Charlotte? How did you persuade them to leave her with you?'

'I intended to bring her back to town. For you to renew your offer, if you so wished.'

'If I wished? Richard, are you crazy? Of course I wish, and Charlotte knows it. But how can we marry if that wretched woman refuses her consent?'

'She won't. Well, are the pair of you betrothed? If so, I suggest we sit and eat some of this excellent fare the landlord has provided. There would have been time for him to roast a capon after all, had he known,' he added reflectively, and Prudence chuckled.

'Well, my love?' Edward asked, and Charlotte, with a shy smile, slipped her hand into his.

'Champagne, mine host!' Lord Mottesford called, and they then explained everything in detail to Edward while they ate.

'I'd no notion you were an heiress,' he said at the end.

'Neither had I, and it feels very strange.'

'But you can't cry off because of it,' Lord Mottesford warned. 'Prudence and I are witnesses.'

'If Charlotte is happy so am I. But it's high time we were setting off for London. Where can Charlotte go?'

'We'll take her to my home,' Prudence said quickly. 'Aunt Lavinia will be delighted to have her until the wedding can be arranged, or Sarah will.'

'Good, so you take Charlotte in your curricle and we will follow when I've settled with the landlord. We'll see you later in Grosvenor Square.'

Edward and Charlotte then left, while Lord Mottesford went to find the landlord. Suddenly, after all the excitement, and alone in the coffee room, Prudence felt oddly bereft. She was sitting on the windowseat, her feet curled underneath her, her chin on her hands, when Lord Mottesford returned.

'Well, are we ready?' she asked brightly, coming to her feet.

'Not for a while. Prudence, my dear, am I forgiven?'

'Forgiven?' she asked, suddenly breathless. 'I ought rather to be thanking you for helping Charlotte, and bringing me with you.'

'Sit down.' He took her hand in his and led her back to the windowseat, then sat beside her, retaining her hand in his.

'My lord?'

'I never intended to marry that wretched girl,' he said, an irrepressible twinkle in his eyes, 'although I confess I did not expect to escape quite so easily.'

Prudence laughed. 'Permit me to say that you were thoroughly unscrupulous, my lord! A farmhouse in Westmorland indeed! And needing to retrench! It would have served you well if she had called your bluff!'

'I don't think there was any fear of that. What Emma wanted was a rich and complaisant husband to pay all her bills, while she queened it in London. I'd have found some other way of getting rid of her if those threats had not worked.'

'Unscrupulous, my lord.'

'Indeed. For I could no more have married her than Charlotte could the deplorable Hubert.'

'But why did you permit them to trap you in the first place? It would have been so easy to deny it, to say that it was all a mistake.'

'But I wanted to make you sorry for me,' he replied, in apparent surprise that she should not already have guessed his motives.

'I?'

'Prudence, we started badly with the stupid wager. I never dreamed that you knew of it, or I would have understood earlier your inexplicable coldness, after I was so sure that you were beginning to return my regard.'

'I was unable to believe that you were sincere,' she said slowly. 'I wanted to, so much, but did not dare.'

'I was sincere after the first couple of days, I think. It took so little time to realise that you were different from the usual simpering misses just out of the schoolroom, that I have been avoiding every time I came to London on leave. I certainly never wished even to flirt with them for more than a few days.'

'You are a confirmed flirt?' she teased, suddenly happy beyond her wildest hopes.

'Utterly,' he agreed, 'and unrepentant. But now I shall always flirt with you. Just with you. Am I forgiven? Will you trust me now?'

Prudence nodded, and sighed as he pulled her towards him, to kiss her gently on the forehead.

'When will you marry me, my darling?' he asked, his voice husky.

'Shall I have to live in Westmorland?' she asked, in a mock solemn voice.

'Only if you displease me. But I would live there with you,' he added as she drew away from him. 'I could not bear to be apart from you.'

'And will you allow me a new gown every year?' she queried anxiously.

'I might manage two. And possibly a bonnet as well, as long as you trim it yourself with all the leftover scraps from the gowns you will make.'

She giggled. 'After threatening Emma with such fierce retrenchment, how will you dare to appear in town, my lord?' she demanded.

'I shall live on your money, of course. You are an heiress, aren't you, or have I been misled?'

'I haven't a penny,' Prudence claimed blithely.

'Oh, dear, how can I get out of this betrothal?' he asked with a worried frown.

'Well, I haven't yet accepted your offer, my lord,' she reminded him.

'So you haven't. What a relief. I shall withdraw the whole scheme unless you immediately start to address me with greater respect, as Richard.'

'But I prefer Dicky,' she said pensively.

'I could even tolerate that from you, my darling,' he said, suddenly serious.

'Richard, no!' she exclaimed, and as Prudence turned her face towards him, he bent his mouth to hers.

It was some time later that, shaken by the glimpse she had been vouchsafed of their mutual passion, Prudence sighed and said that she would be an abandoned wretch if she did not agree to marry him now.

It was very late when they arrived in Grosvenor Square, where Charlotte had been welcomed an hour earlier, and where Edward had been invited to join the Fromes for dinner. As Tanner opened the door and Prudence stepped inside the familiar house, Lord Mottesford at her side, Netta came flying down the stairs.

'There,' she exclaimed, ignoring her mother's protests that she ought to be in the schoolroom having her supper, as Lady Frome emerged from the drawing-room and followed her down. 'I knew they would make it up. Mr Gregory explained that he won the wager within the week. When are you getting married? Can I be a bridesmaid?'

Prudence blushed, glanced up at her smiling aunt and uncle, and found that Richard's arm was about her waist.

'She's marrying me just as soon as we can possibly arrange it,' he said firmly. 'I'm not risking any more ridiculous misunderstandings. And I'm not entering into any more wagers with you, my lad,' he added to Edward. 'Unless it's one to beat you to the altar!'

THE END

We do hope that you have enjoyed reading this large print book.

Did you know that all of our titles are available for purchase?

We publish a wide range of high quality large print books including:
Romances, Mysteries, Classics
General Fiction
Non Fiction and Westerns

Special interest titles available in large print are:
The Little Oxford Dictionary
Music Book, Song Book
Hymn Book, Service Book

Also available from us courtesy of Oxford University Press:
Young Readers' Dictionary
(large print edition)
Young Readers' Thesaurus
(large print edition)

For further information or a free brochure, please contact us at:
Ulverscroft Large Print Books Ltd.,
The Green, Bradgate Road, Anstey,
Leicester, LE7 7FU, England.
Tel: (00 44) **0116 236 4325**
Fax: (00 44) **0116 234 0205**

SUMMER IN HANOVER SQUARE

Charlotte Grey

The impoverished Margaret Lambart is suddenly flung into all the glitter of the Season in Regency London. Suspected by her godmother's nephew, the influential Marquis St. George, of being merely a common adventuress, she has, nevertheless, a brilliant success, and attracts the attentions of the young Duke of Oxford. However, when the Marquis discovers that Margaret is far from wanting a husband he finds he has to revise his estimate of her true worth.